TRIAL
AT THE
FAIRE
THE WINDBORNE SERIES
A PREQUEL NOVELLA

BOOKS BY LAUREL WANROW

The Windborne Series ~ for young adults

Double Rescue (prequel novella)

Trial at the Faire (prequel novella)

The Witch of the Meadows

Guardian of the Pines

Lost Whisperer of the Seas

Keepers of the Sea Cliffs

Solstice Gifts (holiday short story)

The Luminated Threads Series ~ for ages 15 & up

The Unraveling, Volume One

The Twisting, Volume Two

The Binding, Volume Three

The Luminated Threads Volumes 1-3 Box Set

Science Fiction Romance ~ for adults

Passages

TRIAL AT THE FAIRE

THE WINDBORNE SERIES
A PREQUEL NOVELLA

LAUREL WANROW

Sprouting Star Press

To the zoom writing partners who kept each other sane during COVID-19.

THE CHALLENGE OF A TRIAL

The Cairnkin Village Medieval Faire Reenactment, Scotland
Late August, in modern times

"All at once now! Heave!"

Muscles tightening, Raven of the Meadows *heaved* the bulky material from the ground. In the dim morning light, the other fellows did the same around the big tent. Their chaperones ducked inside with the center pole and lifted the roof into a peak. Raven hauled on the nearest rope and trudged away from his side of the limp fabric. The pavilion unfolded and ballooned out. The canvas monstrosity was a round, antiquated-looking thing of stripes, though it was newly made to fit the style of medieval faires.

Magic would have made this task easier, if only they were allowed to use it.

"Hold her there," called Ms. Scallop, a cousin of Raven's grandmother. She came trotting around the pavilion's perimeter, the tail of her triangular shawl flapping at the waist of her ankle-length skirt. She gave his rope a curt nod, loosening gray curls from her kerchief as she swung away. "Gentlemen, you may install the framing spokes!" Ms. Scallop directed the adults from the tent's doorway, then turned to the youths again. "Quick, lasses, get these ropes staked!"

Raven hung on to his rope, keeping it taut. *Please, let it be Willow who comes to my side.*

Hammering rang out all around them on the grounds of the old house. Other faire vendors rushed about, unloading crates and tables from automobiles and setting up tents, though none was as colorful as Ms. Scallop's pink and blue curiosity.

This faire seemed to be a big to-do, even larger than their gatherings at home on the Isle of Giuthas. Cairnkin Village apparently held its medieval faire every August on the grounds of its historic manor house. Raven had learned about it only a few weeks ago. This was a human place, on human land, and not the kind of affair the Windborne paid any mind to.

Well, most Windborne. Gran's cousin Scallop made her living selling her spun woolens to humans. She was one of the few Windborne he'd heard of who actually lived on human land. He thought she was mad to live here and forever conceal her powers. Sadly, Gran didn't agree. When she'd learned about this faire and how people dressed up in historic costumes and tried to mimic the speech of their ancestors, she'd decided it'd be the perfect trial for the isle's youths to test their skills at not being detected as wizards.

Raven, however, was more worried about winning Willow's approval than he was about passing the trial, and he planned to spend as much time with her today as possible.

As if he'd magicked his wish into being, Willow of the Forest appeared around the pavilion, her blond hair blowing loose in the wind. Her long, pink dress reminded him of the apple blossoms that bloomed on the isle, and indeed, it had flowers embroidered over it, blue, green and a yellow that matched her amber eyes.

They'd been lifelong friends, but somehow earlier this

summer he'd noticed her more. The way she walked, the way her hair always looked so soft... He was taken with the urge to catch a lock of it now and tell her how he admired it so much that he'd been growing his own hair longer. Instead, he smiled at her. "At least we won't have a hard time finding her booth again." He gestured to the rows of plainer, solid-color pavilions going up on either side and across from them. "Outrageous colors, huh?"

Willow glanced up. "I like it. We never have anything as pretty at home."

Blast. He'd blown it. Already. "I, uh, aye, it works." *By the Orb, have you nothing better to say?* Practically the first thing he'd uttered to her today, and he'd sounded like a git.

Flipping her skirt out of the way, Willow dropped near his feet, shoved a stake into the grass and hammered, doing an impressive job, too, especially considering it was by hand. Luckily, their wizard mentors had trained them to do things physically, for those times when Windborne magic was short. Or for when they might be among nonmagical humans.

Once Willow was done, she took the end of his rope and tied it around the stake. She rose and smiled up at him. Then she tugged a strand of his shoulder-length hair. "Your hair has grown quite long."

He swallowed. Did he dare tell her? *She seems to care for me more than the other fellows, but maybe that's all in my head?*

"Its length fits right in with the other dressed-up fairegoers, and soon you'll be able to tie it back," she said. "I've never seen you wear this shirt before either."

Blessed Orb, she'd noticed. For a moment, all he could do was grin and smooth his hands down the oversize brown dress shirt with the stand-up collar and lacings at the throat. "'Tis my dad's. Gran said if I pulled it in with a belt"—he tucked his thumbs behind the leather—"it'd pass for a tunic." He'd matched the belt to his knee boots and tucked his trousers into them. Half the crafters' clothes weren't as authentic-looking as their dressier Windborne clothing.

Willow nodded. "You'd think Lady Lark has been to one of these faires before."

He and Willow were alone, just the two of them between the high canvas walls. This was his chance. "Will you take a turn with me when we're sent off to buy food? I think I've got their coins figured out, but I don't want to lose any of my trade credit—"

"It's simple tens." Coral of the Seas barreled around the side of the tent, brown braids swinging and knee boots showing beneath the hem of her blue skirt. "A hundred pence to a pound. The coins have the amounts on them. Surely you can keep that in your head?" The younger—and much shorter—lass reached up to tap Raven's cheek, but he lurched back.

"Coral, I swear—"

"Ah-ah!" She shook a finger at him, all the while grinning smugly. "Careful. Wouldn't want your temper to"—she leaned closer— "show."

He darted a look at his hands. No glow.

Coral giggled.

The little stinker. He loomed over her. "Just wait until we're back on the isle," he muttered so only she could hear.

"Aye." She winked, not at all intimidated by his greater height. "Just wait." She knelt, dampening her skirt in the wet grass, and tugged at the knot Willow had tied. "Blimey, Willow! A granny knot? This will never hold!" In a trice, she had it undone—

Raven reached to catch the loosening rope just as Coral yanked it tight, and the friction burned his finger. He kept his grunt to himself.

Coral retied it. "Thank the... Um, *good thing* Lady Lark sent me around to check them."

"Oh dear," Willow said. "Redo my other, please." She

grasped Coral's arm and steered her around the tent's perimeter.

Raven followed a few steps behind. He could go along and hold the rope, though Coral would overrun the conversation again and get in more digs at him. Before he was close enough, Willow clasped the rope and held the section of the tent upright as well as he could have. *Right, chap, the lass is more than capable, magically and physically.* Even Coral was.

He'd spent many sleepless nights listing reasons Willow would refuse to try a prebond trial with him, the courting agreement in which teens could also test how their magic worked together. She had far more experience in caring for her habitat than he did—she'd been learning the care of the Forest from her mother since eighth year, while he'd begun his apprenticeship at the customary tenth year. She remembered every spell she ever learned, while he had to practice repeatedly. To his knowledge, she'd never angered a single elder...unlike him. His latest mishap at the start of summer—a complete accident, and the bird was progressing fine now!—had put him under the scrutiny of every elder at any lesson.

Why would she be interested in prebonding with me when I have such a rotten reputation?

Raven rechecked his fingers, though there'd been no sign of magic. After the elders had threatened them with months of a quash—a grounding of their magic—if they showed anything magical in this human village, he'd locked his energy out of his hands. Even so, he hadn't gone as far as to lock it away in its storage cores. He wasn't a child. At fifteenth year, he could control his magic, thank the Or—

Argh! No doubt, he, of any of them, would get in trouble for spouting a Windborne curse.

If he wanted to fix his reputation, he ought to start with passing this trial at fitting in among human society. Which meant he couldn't get into one bit of trouble today. Aside from no use of magic, the trial tasks were easy enough: help Ms. Scallop with her craft sales and lambs, talk to strangers in a human manner and purchase food. No mention of magic, use of magical terms or references to any of their Windborne doings. He simply had to pay attention to everything he said and did.

Skirting around the tent in the opposite direction from Willow—though that was the last thing he wanted to do—Raven returned to Ms. Scallop's wagon, where the others from the isle were unloading the spinning wheel and woolen goods.

Among the group, Beri swung around with a crate, his movement sending his rusty-red hair flying up. Upon seeing Raven, he wrinkled his freckled nose. *About time you joined us,* he thought-spoke. *Get your mooning in?*

Beri? snapped Dad.

Eyes widening, Beri froze, then darted his gaze over his shoulder. At the front of the wagon, Raven's dad, Merlin, and Gran were both staring.

Blast. Beri had mistakenly used their family channel instead of privately sending the message. He and Beri might not be true brothers, but they'd become just as close in the seven years since Beri's parents died. Dad was equally strict with both of them, and now his eyebrows went up in a warning.

Undoubtedly, they weren't supposed to be sending messages at all. But Dad hadn't told them to shut down their thought-speaking channels.

Gran beckoned them over to the space next to a fence and hedgerow where Ms. Scallop's horses were tied.

Blast, blast, blast. Maybe she'd meant only Beri? As Beri put down the crate and walked back, Gran continued to stare at Raven.

He went, too. They might cajole Dad, but never Gran, the opposite of what most folks expected of a gray-haired woman barely five feet tall. Today, she wore one of her yellow-green homemade dresses topped by an apron, shawl and a fancy old cloak pin in a decent imitation of a medieval costume.

Beside tiny Gran, Dad towered above them at over six feet tall. He held the leads of four lambs they'd brought for visitors to pet, fitting in perfectly with this faire in his leather trousers and vest. He'd trimmed his black beard and tied back his long hair.

When Raven and Beri stopped before them, Gran leaned forward and waited until they ducked their heads to hers. "No private conversations," she hissed. "Act human."

"Do as Lark says," said Dad. "None of...*that*."

"Aye, sir. Sorry, ma'am," Beri mumbled and threw Raven a glare.

"S'not my fault," Raven snapped back. "Sheesh, you're not happy about it, but since we're here, make an effort to have fun, would you?" At Dad's look, he shut his mouth. They'd all been telling Beri to relax. He knew.

"We will discuss it at home." Gran sliced her hand through the air to end the conversation. A metal chain glinted beneath her shifting shawl when she moved.

Raven hesitated. *Did I really see that?*

She gestured toward the wagon. "Could you lads take the pen panels for the lambs and set them up at the tent? Then return to settle the animals with their hay."

When her shawl moved again, Raven saw the familiar chain slipping from her neck. "Gran?" he whispered. "Something is broken. Are you wearing..." How could he say this without speaking any forbidden words? "An extra *necklace?*"

Gran patted her neckline, and as her fingers found the chain ends and traced a rod-shaped lump, her eyes grew wide. She glanced around, then drew Raven toward her side like a shield. Nodding to Beri, she moved close to Dad despite the lambs scampering around his legs. Beri stepped into place on the fourth side to completely enclose the four of them.

"I, uh…" Gran drew a shuddering breath. "I canna believe it. I seem to have forgotten to leave…*it* at Scallop's house. And now the chain is broken. What should I do?" She clutched a fold of fabric wrapping her fallen peregrinator, a magical traveling device that was definitely forbidden to carry outside of their Windborne enclave.

Curses. They'd covered this in their preparation lessons. If a magical device got lost in the human world, the wizard responsible would face more than their enclave council. The breach would go to the Windborne's Department of Magical Regulation, and the DMR didn't take magical leaks lightly. The entire enclave would be restricted from travel until a review had been made. But Gran's device wasn't lost. It was just…out. Raven couldn't think. He certainly couldn't joke. This was serious, adult territory.

Beri leaned in. "Perhaps I should fetch Ms. Scallop. She lives among them. She would know what to do." At Dad's nod, he was off.

In minutes, he'd brought back Ms. Scallop. She carried a wad of wool and a paper envelope in her hand and a tote bag slung over her shoulder.

"Wrap it in here." Ms. Scallop thrust the wool at Gran. "We shall secure it in one of my sample envelopes and keep it in the cashbox for safety. Someone will be with the box at all times."

They surrounded Gran again while she nestled the broken chain and the three-inch-long glass rod—it had yellow-green swirls throughout it, the same color as Gran's magic—in the wool and did as her cousin had said. Ms. Scallop locked the envelope in the bottom of her slender metal cashbox and returned it to her bag. She gave Gran a consoling hug. "Nothing need be said."

Well, that didn't seem as safe as Gran carrying the device in her pocket, but Raven wasn't an elder. What did he know?

Dad put a hand to each of their shoulders. "Lads, our family is done with mishaps for the day. Best get back to setting up."

"Aye," Beri murmured, and they turned to go.

Raven grinned. "Yep, I'm ready to move on." To Willow and spending time with her. He spotted her across the car park, returning on the path from the crafters' tents.

His ready smile slid off.

Willow was walking back with Salm of the Seas. That wasn't unusual. They were supposed to stay together. And Salm, Coral's seventeenth-year brother, was jabbering on in his typical carefree way. Only this time, he was leaning down for the conversation, with a most attentive tilt to his head *and* his hand at Willow's elbow.

What is going on there?

2

HANG THE STUDY OF HUMAN DIFFERENCES

Beri unloaded the pen panels from the wagon bed with Raven's help and divided the fencing between them. He hoisted up his half and checked the crafter car park for moving automobiles. A few new ones had parked at the far end, but the way was clear. They needed to go now. Yet Raven hadn't picked up his panels. He was restacking them while looking around.

Was there a problem?

Across the field, people called to each other and laughed loudly in the still morning. Their automobile and trailer doors creaked and banged. It was bloody hard to tell if there was a problem.

Stick together, they'd been told. *Help each other out.*

Every action on this day had to be planned and careful. Beri had protested leaving the safety of their enclave from the moment the elders announced this field trip, but Merlin wouldn't hear of his staying home. Merlin had advised him to *enjoy* the human festival and *study* the differences in the humans' lives.

Spells! He already knew how their unnatural machinery took the lives of others. Why couldn't Merlin understand? He'd survived one brief visit earlier this summer, but the elders said it dinnae count for this "human experience" trial. He and Raven had spent most of that visit with animals. So he was here now, and he fully intended to meet each expectation for this trial's completion. He would *nae* be returning to human land again. It was too dangerous.

"The lambs," hissed Beri, his shoulders tight. "Merlin is waiting."

Raven was still messing around with rearranging the top panel.

His fingers growing stiff around the metal wires, Beri checked for automobiles once more. He likely wouldn't be breaking the rules to leave Raven here, because the tent was visible from the wagon, but he didn't want to risk getting into trouble. Plus, he was nae about to miss the opportunity of Salm and Willow being on the path, an extra layer of safety. "Will you come on?" he growled.

Raven shook his head. "I'll catch up."

Beri marched away. Merlin had already chastised him for the use of magic. He didn't need to be reprimanded for punching Raven, too.

And he sorely wanted to. More people headed for the crafter area. Beri kept an eye on their movements, staying back to allow a crafter with a squeaky-wheeled wagon to go first on the path. That whine, thuds of boots, constant talking, hammering... The noise of this press of people had been only a slight worry, until he'd realized their buzz blocked the sound of the automobiles.

Ahead, Willow and Salm walked slowly toward him, whispering as they looked with wide eyes at the passersby. Could any of the humans tell they were being studied? Beri didn't detect a one of them gazing back. People were too busy setting up.

Salm and Willow stopped as he reached them.

"Beri, my mate," Salm said, "keep watch for the pirate. I am quite jealous of his felt and feathered hat."

Beri nodded and made to head on before Willow caught his arm. Spells. What now?

"Salm? Go ahead to the wagon," she said. "I'll be there soon."

Salm started to protest, then did as Willow said. Beri walked on. He didn't like the set of Willow's mouth. She was kind, but very nearly copied her mother in mothering both him and Raven...though Willow had a different interest with Raven. Beri could tell.

She kept pace with him. "How are you feeling?"

She knew, of course. *Everyone* knew he hadn't wanted to come. And why. "I canna stop thinking of my mum now that we are here on human land." He didn't look at her as he said it. "The automobiles..."

"Her death," Willow said with simple straightforwardness.

Each sight of an automobile reminded him of the day he'd been told his mum wasn't returning home from a rare trip to a human city. "I..." He stopped. He hadn't thought of his mum this intensely in years, and his sadness added to his worry. No matter that he and Willow had grown up closely on the isle, Beri couldn't say a word more and stay dry-eyed.

"'Tis all right to feel your pain." Willow patted his arm. "I'm sorry. Is there anything I can do?"

Was there? He wanted to know if he stepped from a busy street corner like his mum had, would he live, when she hadn't? It sounded ridiculous to even think it, let alone voice his worry. He had to listen for the motors himself. "Nay, nothing," he murmured.

"Let me know if anything comes to mind."

He was able to smile in reply. She was a true friend. She'd gotten him and Raven out of many fixes, like the time their rope swing had broken a branch, and she'd not only caught them, but also repaired the limb. Still, nothing could fix your mum's dying. Having Willow acknowledge his hurt helped, especially with Raven so easygoing about this trip. Growing up, they'd shared everything. Now Raven had different plans, different worries. Beri wasn't jealous, but he missed Raven's distractions.

Beri dropped off his panels and returned to the wagon. Willow and Coral stood at the back with Raven. Willow elbowed Raven's arm and whispered something, and Beri knew they'd been talking about him. Around the front of the wagon, Merlin still had the lambs by their leads and was speaking with Salm. Had he noticed that Raven hadn't left to help set up the lamb pen?

Beri kept his annoyance to himself, but he was nae about to carry the second set of panels.

Up in the wagon, Oyster of the Estuary bent double behind crates of woolens. His daily swims gave him the muscles to power through anything—including shoving two double-stacked crates, one per hand. The boxes skidded to the back of the wagon, their bouncing skeins of yarn matching his curly, sandy-colored hair.

Before Beri could reach for one of the boxes, Salm arrived and took the closest. He tossed Beri a glare.

What is that about?

As Salm departed, Coral leaned around Willow. "Why is Salm mad? I haven't done anything this time."

"That, a fellow doesn't need to ask," Raven answered. "He's been carrying boxes while you tie pretty knots."

"Ha," Beri said to Coral. "I'd love to let you take the blame, but he aimed that look at me, and I haven't done anything either."

"Shh," Willow admonished. "Everyone is doing their part."

Oyster squatted before them. "I thought he was mad at me. Last week, he flew—*came* down to the Estuary with the dolphins to swim with me like usual. But when I tried to help Willow carry the tent poles earlier, he got huffy and asked what I was doing."

Raven froze, his eyes narrowing. "What *were* you doing?" he snapped.

Spells, what had set Raven off?

Before Beri could elbow Raven, Oyster jumped down and picked up a crate. "Not half of what I should be, according to Mother."

"Hey." Coral pointed to the crates remaining at the head of the wagon. "Aren't you going to pass us the rest?"

Without looking back, Oyster left. Beri grabbed a crate and hurried after him. Being the tallest of the lads, he caught up quickly. Oyster, who might surpass Willow in proper behavior, didn't deserve Raven's attitude, whatever had brought it on. "Ignore those two and enjoy today."

Oyster side-eyed him. "*You* are telling me this?"

"Well, someone ought to enjoy it."

"Mother agrees with you that this is a dangerous exercise. Lady Lark had to pressure her to allow me to attend."

"Better with support than thrust into a situation with no experience," Beri parroted Merlin's reasoning.

"Mother agreed," Oyster said dryly. "Yet the only ones of us who have our minds on the task are me, you and Willow. The other three regard this as a frolic."

Beri shook his head. "Salm has passed this trial previously. He's come along to help."

"So his sister could attend, you mean. Coral is too young to be here," Oyster said firmly. "Mother says the elders have erred in that decision."

Flights. Some days, talking to Oyster was like dealing with Dr. Jekyll and Mr. Hyde as he wavered between trying to please his mother and being himself. "Have you considered that the very things you don't like your mother doing to you, you are doing to others? Like judging Coral."

Oyster huffed and stopped walking. Beri nearly slammed into him.

"Sp—" Beri started and caught himself, for across their path came a woman wearing a wool vest with lacings over a full skirt. Her green hands cradled a lidded pewter mug as if it were treasure.

Oyster stared at her green face, his eyes wide.

Spells, indeed. Beri had to admit—only to himself—that his guard had gone down. He needed that for automobiles. This...*person* was fine, even if she had unaccountably tinted her skin. No danger there.

Behind her strode a man, also with green skin and wearing a laced-up vest, but one decidedly too small over his linen shirt and cutoff trousers. He carried a babe swaddled in an oversize knit jumper with a simple linen cap. Neither of their clothing choices was too odd, just the flared tubes—mimicking mushrooms?—protruding from the man's bald head.

"What was that?" Oyster whispered after they had passed.

Beri shook his head and whispered back, "Best not to question why hu—they do these things."

Oyster studied him a moment before starting forward again. "To judge, you mean."

Good, Oyster was on board now. "One of the challenges of the trial is to support each other in all the ways *people* do." That was the way elders said *without magic.* "As you surmised, 'tis my goal to accomplish our tasks, nae repeat them." *And never return.*

Oyster sighed. "Mine, too. Mother will be furious if I have to repeat the trial in three years with the twelfth-years. That would be an embarrassment." They were approaching Ms. Scallop's tent when he said, "Very well. I shall do what I can to make sure each of us succeeds. I will be the kind of friend you are to me."

"I...thank you. I daresay you have reminded me to do the same."

"Willow said..." Oyster ducked his head. "I mean, seems you're holding up fine."

Aye, Willow had told the others. He was managing now,

but... Beri's gaze swept to the busy entrance gate where more automobiles kept arriving.

"If you decide you need an excuse," Oyster said, "how about sick to your stomach?"

"Tried that already." Beri shook his head. "Merlin suggested taking castor oil, and I became miraculously better. I'm sure he wouldn't hesitate to *discover* he's brought it along. Besides, I have to pass the trial."

Oyster laughed. "Clearly, you don't have the proper practice at this. Do everything you need to pass *before* you become ill. With a *reason*. Some strange food they serve here is sure to set you off."

'Twas nae a bad idea.

Smiling, Oyster winked in a knowing way. "Manage that, and you will be the golden lad. Among all in our group, I fear Raven is the one most likely to fail."

Aye? He was distracted, all right—especially with Beri's mistake of using magic and Lark's forgotten peregrinator—but he did care about passing, Beri was sure about that. Almost as much as he cared about Willow...

Oh Blessed Orb. That explained why Raven was rude to Oy *and* why Salm had glared at him. Salm had been showering attention on Willow, and then Willow had broken off to talk to him. Ho, did Raven know Salm had Willow in his sights?

Beri laughed humorlessly. "Raven has many things on his mind today. Take my advice and help where you can, but don't jeopardize your own trial. That's what I'm doing."

3

VYING FOR AN OPPORTUNITY

Ms. Scallop was far more particular about those brown lambs than Raven had realized. After he'd carried over his pen panels, Gran's cousin put him to installing fasteners to hold them together, four to a joint. Beri conveniently claimed he needed to keep walking to work off his nerves, leaving Raven alone on his knees in the wet grass.

"I canna risk them escaping," Ms. Scallop repeated as she joined an adjacent set of panels, and Dad continued to hold the leads—not Willow, as Raven had suggested. "Five years of breeding has paid off with this lot."

From their family visits to her farm, Raven knew she nurtured a breed that wasn't all crossed and mixed for some human reason. These sheep were still like their wild ancestors from a human island, and there was something unusual about their long, fancy horns.

He finished the fifth set of fasteners and rose up, plucking loose the soaked fabric of his trousers.

With the bag holding the cashbox swinging at her middle, Ms. Scallop once more shoved and tried twisting apart the two newly attached panels. They held. She nodded. "You do a job right, Raven."

"Thanks." Hmm, wet knees didn't seem so bad now. It was a small price, he supposed, given Ms. Scallop had helped Gran and not said a word while protecting the peregrinator. As they knelt to install another panel, he asked, "What's special about these lambs? Do the horns make the buyers think the wool is better quality?"

She laughed. "Ach, the wool *is* of the highest quality, and I suppose you're correct, folks are drawn to it more if they can say it came from a scarce six-horned sheep."

"Six?" He glanced at the lambs. Some of their horn nubs showed, but maybe the wool covered others?

"Two of them!" Her eyes gleamed proudly. "And the other two Manx Loaghtans have four."

"Most sheep only have two, right?"

She nodded. "Aye, these'd fetch a pretty price, but I'm keeping them to build my flock. I'll show you which they are once we can turn them loose in here."

They finished the pen and put in their hay, water and an old blanket over one end for a hide. Dad let the lambs free. Two of them did indeed have three sets of bumpy horn nubs buried in their soft fleece. Raven repeated the *Manx Loaghtan* name he'd have to know to answer folks' questions.

"I'll keep an eye on them while we set up," Ms. Scallop said. "Would you move the display racks inside the tent?"

Raven joined the others hauling crate after crate for Ms. Scallop, until they had her spinning and sales displays set up. Then he carried crates for any of the neighboring crafters that his gran deemed needed a hand. All of the Giuthas youths helped, dispersed to this trailer or that, in pairs that Gran directed. Raven hustled around with Beri or Oyster or Coral, but not Willow. When would his turn with her come? *How can I casually ask what she was laughing about with Salm?* When he saw Salm with her *again*, it sank in that their continued pairing was no accident.

"Salm is seeking Willow's affection," he hissed to Beri as they wove through the increasing parade of humans.

"I, uh, had noticed." Beri wrinkled his nose. "Willow won't take him seriously."

"Are you sure?"

Lips pressed together, Beri shook his head.

Blast it all! Beri knew Willow as well as Raven did. If Beri didn't know whether Willow was taking Salm seriously, then Raven had no idea. The three of them were close, but that didn't mean that the rest of the kids on the isle weren't close friends, too. There were only the six of them, for Orb's sake. What if Salm—who could be too charming for his own good—actually asked Willow to prebond? Salm wouldn't hesitate to ask a serious thing like that. He...he might do it anytime. Like...today.

The fear that Salm might get to Willow first—and she would say yes!—wouldn't leave Raven's mind. *Then...I must declare myself. As soon as possible.*

Over an hour later, Gran felt, at last, they had done enough service.

"Where's Beri?" Dad asked him. "We have some reminders before you head out."

He found Beri inside the tent, slouched in a chair. Raven kicked his foot. "What's with you?"

"'Tis becoming too blasted crowded out there," he muttered. "Gonna spend the rest of the trip right here."

"Like Gran will let you do that. Buck up." He slid an arm under Beri's and hoisted him to his feet.

Outside, their chaperones had everyone gathered.

"Stay together, threes or pairs," Dad reminded them. "Engage in three or more conversations. The point of your trial is to gain confidence around these people. Each of you should ask a hu—"

"Someone," interjected Mr. Grouse, another of their chaperones.

"Someone," Dad repeated, "for information or directions. Even if you don't need directions." He gave Beri a pointed look.

Beri didn't meet his gaze, so Dad repeated it, saying his name, to which Beri muttered, "Aye."

Dad shifted his gaze to Raven.

Raven jerked a thumb toward Beri. "I am nae responsible for him."

Beri's head snapped around. "I do nae need looking after. I ken my duties."

"Ye all are responsible for each other," Dad said firmly.

"Aye, scallywags," Salm said with a grin. "Me ma gave me the same orders regarding Coral, worrying over the minnow. I'll trade any one of you for her."

His sister backhanded his belly, but Salm, grinning broader, caught it and spun the small lass in a twirl, making all of them —except Beri—laugh.

Gran shoved her way among the group. "The lot of you are wasting time and scaring away Scallop's customers by loitering about. Do as ye are told and be off until Scallop's demonstration begins. One hour." She flipped her hands in a shooing motion.

Raven backed away automatically, but this time Gran's flick hadn't come with her usual spark of magical incentive to abide by her orders. He grinned down at her, which he quite enjoyed now that he'd passed her in height. "I could like this place if that's how orders are given here."

Gran eyed him. "Remember, my lad, you will be going home again."

Behind her, Dad frowned. They shooed.

Raven darted around the others to make sure he was beside Willow. They wove past the crafters' tents, newly opened food stalls and an empty performance stage. Not much was going on yet. The end of the vendor area opened onto an open space leading up to the grand manor house, a fancy stone structure with crenelated watchtowers. Most of the long lawn had been roped off, and inside, several chaps were setting out open wooden fencing in a long row to divide the lawn.

Salm hailed a passerby in modern human clothing. "This demonstration thing, is it worth watching?"

"The joust?" The woman shrugged. "First time here myself, but I heard it's the main event everyone comes to see. It'll be crowded."

"Then we shall attend. Thank you, milady!" Salm made a small, elegant bow. It came off perfectly in his best leather waistcoat and trousers tucked into polished knee boots. When the lady smiled, he sauntered on, Coral and Willow in his wake.

Blast, he'd lost Willow to Salm again. Raven elbowed Beri. "Trust Salm to show up the rest of us." He wouldn't admit that Salm had looked fully at ease while putting on his act. He had the most experience of any of them talking to folks, since the Seas family traveled to different enclaves to monitor fisheries and exchange goods for everyone. He'd also completed trials among humans with his older sisters, so he was the only one of them to have permission to go about alone today. *Please, let him.* That might be the only way Raven could garner more time with Willow.

Beri hadn't answered. When Raven glanced over, his adopted brother's jaws were clenched and his forehead creased. Raven should heed the usual signals to keep his mouth shut. Salm was his problem, not Beri, and he needed to keep it that way.

When they caught up, Salm said, "That, mates, is how it's done. Beri?" Salm gestured to a couple consulting a brochure.

"No need," he snapped. "I know what a joust is and can see it's nae started." In long strides, Beri took off fast enough that everyone except Salm had to trot to keep him in sight. Beri trekked along the rope bordering the expansive lawn, headed for a line of trees on the far side.

Beri wasn't usually so abrupt—this place must be worrying him as much as he'd claimed it would.

One of the costumed workers carrying fencing saw them. "Looking for the coffee and doughnuts? Service is up on the side patio." He lifted his chin in the direction of the house.

Coffee and doughnuts? What was he talking about? Raven glanced at Beri, but he was waving to the chap.

"Thanks, mate," Beri called. "Will the jousting start soon?"

"Nah, not until nine. However, the maze out back is open." Again, he nodded toward the house. "Quiet right now. Give it a go."

Spells. For the fellow who hadn't wanted to come, Beri was now ahead of everyone in completing his trial assignment. Raven met Willow's gaze.

Her brows rose. "Did he—"

"Brilliant!" Beri answered, stuffed his hands in his pockets and strolled in that direction.

With a glance toward Willow, Salm saluted the bloke before grinning around at them. He gestured them forward and took the lead from Beri.

Blast that showoff! Yet a few paces on, Raven had it. A maze was perfect. He could split off with Willow and ask her if she'd prebond with him. She'd know how he felt. He'd know her answer, and they could enjoy the rest of the day…

If she said she wanted to. Oh great bloody—

"Look at the colors!" Coral exclaimed.

They'd arrived at a table covered in boxes filled with round cakes iced in a rainbow of brightness. Strangely, every one of them had a hole in the center.

"What'll it be, guys?" asked a fellow of about their age manning the table. "Just doughnuts, or coffee, too?" He held up a paper cup, every finger bearing a ring, smiled and cocked his purple-haired head at a jaunty angle.

The others debated this coffee thing while deciding on which doughnut. Raven picked a chocolate one covered in coconut, though he didn't see how he could eat with his jittery stomach. Salm and Oyster agreed to the drink with their doughnuts.

"Way to go, mates!" The lad took their coins and passed over the steaming cups.

They walked off a few paces. The coffee smelled suspicious. Salm downed it with gusto, and Oyster pursed his lips as if he'd been betrayed. Doughnuts, on the other hand—

Raven and Beri groaned simultaneously at the first bite. "Do you suppose Merlin can extend his baking to this?" Beri asked.

"One can hope," Raven mumbled around the sweetness melting in his mouth. "How do they get them crunchy on the outside?"

"Oh Blessed…" Willow covered her mouth while the rest of them laughed at her near slip. She delicately wiped her fingers on the paper that had held her doughnut. "Whatever it is they say here. That was delicious."

"Blimey, 'twas!" Coral licked the sugar from her fingers. "I could eat another—wait. I can!" She dug in the little bag she had slung across her shoulder and extracted a handful of coins.

Raven just wanted to get back to walking beside Willow, Beri on her other side, like they always did at home. Then he'd have a chance to get her away from Salm.

Coral tugged on Salm's arm. "Can you come—"

"Get someone else." He shook her off. "I plan to beat all of you to the center of the maze." Not too distant, a solid hedge of boxwood blocked the view beyond the back of the house.

"I'd like another holey cake," said Oyster. "That lad taking the money was…interesting."

"Agreed." Coral grinned. "Worth another look."

Raven lunged and grabbed each of their arms. "No can do,"

he said firmly. "Since Salm can go off alone, we've got to split up to beat him at this maze. We still have time to do it. You two and Beri head left once we're inside. Willow and I will take the right. One of our teams will surely top him."

"Ha!" Salm fell for the challenge and took off running toward a gap in the hedge marked as the entrance.

Coral hooted and gave chase, Beri beside her. Oyster passed them in a sprint like when his mother had caught him shirtless last year during a heatwave.

And as simple as that, Raven had Willow to himself.

They trotted together, turning right, then left at the end of a long corridor, left and left again, threading their way deeper and deeper. Raven didn't think the giddy feeling taking over his head was strictly from zigzagging. Several times, he caught Willow looking at him when he'd glanced at her. Did that mean what he hoped it did?

Willow slowed at an intersection. "Toward the middle, that would be more rights, would it not?"

"Not necessarily. Could be that's how they trick you."

They took the left. At the next, their pause made his fluttering insides too much to bear. He looked both ways down the empty corridor and, on a whim, pointed upward. "I could do a little spy hop up and check."

Willow rapped his chest. "You wouldn't dare!"

At her touch, his heart pounded harder. "I would." He managed to wink, to keep up the joking. "Only if I were alone. Wouldn't want you to be in trouble."

She rolled her eyes. "Kind of you." She gave him a light push and once more ran to the left, clearly away from the center.

He hadn't thought it'd be that complicated of a maze, but... Could she also purposefully be avoiding the others? He jogged after her, catching up and running with her, step in step.

"Maybe it's a kindness to myself," he said. "I'd miss you if you were restricted to your house. Or worse, quashed!"

She grinned up at him. "'Tis far more likely that you would be the one quashed, and I'd miss you, too. It's not much fun having only my little brothers to talk to."

The excitement in Raven's gut churned into a heavy weight. A comparison to brothers—and younger ones at that!—was not good. He ventured a cautious, "No?"

Willow shook her head. "You only see them in short spurts, and they adore you. Me, they challenge at every turn, though I am in charge when Mam and Poppa must work. It'll only get worse once Mam has the baby, and she's sure it will be a boy, too." She gave him a sideways glance.

Ach, once the new baby came, he wouldn't be seeing her as much. Well, this was typical of her worries, and at least she wasn't comparing him to Beri. She was at her mother's call only if she was at home... "You should apply to the council for an independent shelter on your trial area, as Beri and I have."

"Neither of my trial areas has an existing shelter, not like yours."

True, the hollow in the Pines grove was perfect, one of the reasons they'd chosen it for a trial. "We'll help you find one. Given all the land the Forest contains, there must be one. Or we can construct something, as another trial."

She met his glance with a soft smile. "I accept your assistance."

"Brilliant," he breathed.

At the next corner, they hit a dead end and had to backtrack. Willow slowed, declaring, "I'm getting turned around. Let's approach this more methodically."

"We should," he agreed while his head said, *Do it. Ask her now.*

Between the boxwood walls, the air was still and fragrant, the only sounds the birds chirping beyond. They walked slowly, side by side, not speaking. Every time he glanced at her, Willow seemed to be looking at him, then they'd look away at the same time. This was it, his chance. Raven checked before and behind them. Deserted. He wiped his sweaty palms down his trousers. "I wonder…"

He stopped to steady his voice.

Willow stopped, too. "Something wrong?" She stepped closer and peered up at him.

"Naught." Orb, he was rattled. But then, Willow noticed everything. "Do you think you might—"

Footsteps pounded, growing louder. They whirled around and separated from each other just before Coral and Salm rounded the corner.

"Time to go!" Coral sang out. "Ms. Scallop's demonstration is soon. Oyster and Beri headed back already. How did you two get stuck far away in this dead-end corner?"

"Coral, no time for chatting!" Salm waved a hand to cut her off. "Willow is the only one who knows the woolens."

Willow started forward. "Oh, aye. Direct us out, please." She gripped Salm's elbow.

Raven's heart sank. *It should be me she's touching!* His chance was gone.

4

PLAYING AT HUMAN

Wanting to blast an energy ball into something, Raven followed Willow and Salm between the maze hedges, the scent of boxwood now overpowering. He couldn't have worse luck, losing this chance, and with Salm of the Seas ready to grab Willow's attention at every turn and snatch her out of Raven's reach!

"So?" Coral trod at his heels. "Why were you two back here? Alone?"

He slammed to a stop and pivoted—

The slight lass lunged out of range, smashing against the foliage, fingers spread. Ready. At her grin, his energy rose in his channels, and it took the grip of an eagle on a thrashing salmon for him to contain it.

"Why," Raven ground out, "do you find the most inopportune moments to hound me with the bloodiest, inanest questions?" He spun and raced after the others. If it wouldn't get him quashed, he'd magic the pesky lass to stay lost in the maze.

Outside the tall hedges, humans crowded the walkways that'd been empty before, flooding in from the direction of the car park. Salm led the way among the people and around the great house.

Casting a glance back to make sure Coral was following—they had to stay together despite what he wished—Raven wove around a family and caught up to Willow. She'd let loose of Salm, and Raven wanted to take her hand as they had when they were younger, but he also wanted his hands free in case they needed to defend themselves.

Nae! *What are you thinking, you git?* This bout of nerves was simply from listening to Beri's rants. Humans might be somewhat different than Windborne, but not that much. This was exactly the test the elders had set forth for them—to be comfortable and inconspicuous among humans. He'd pass the trial, because he wanted Willow to know he had. *That* meant more to him than any approval from the elders.

They passed queues for the fragrant, strange foods, jugglers waltzing around, a musical group tuning their instruments, little kids being herded into a line and issued swords—

Willow stumbled to a halt, bringing the four of them to a standstill while she stared at the knight demonstrating a weapon swing.

"How is this safe?" Coral hissed.

"I think...aye," Willow whispered. "The swords are pretend. A soft substance."

Salm leaned down to her. "Foam. Our dolphin harnesses are padded with it."

Raven reached between the girls and poked Salm in the back. "I thought you said we must hurry?" The sooner they were done with their turn at watching the booth, the sooner he could find another opportunity to have Willow alone again.

Within the rows of crafters, the people thinned, and the brightly striped tent loomed to their right. Oyster stood at the doorway and, spotting them, called to someone inside. Ms. Scallop appeared at the door as they arrived.

"Not busy yet, thank the stars. Beri has gotten the lesson with the cashbox. Willow dear, please answer any questions about the spinning, plies and laundering. The labels have the breeds of sheep, including my Manx Loaghtans. Do we have everything, dears?"

This last was directed at Oyster and Coral. Oyster lifted Ms. Scallop's compact spinning wheel, and Gran had come out with a basket of spinning supplies that she handed to Coral. Ms. Scallop carried another and led the way to the crafters' stage.

Willow went into the tent with Gran, and Raven followed her. This wasn't the time to ask her what was in his heart, but he could chat. Before he could think of what to say, she took a drop spindle and a basket of fluffy wool and went back out to stand under the awning of the tent. He followed her out, and so did Gran.

"All set?" Gran asked everyone. "Be welcoming to customers, not talking amongst yourselves. Plenty of time for that when you are nae working."

Argh. Raven nodded like Gran expected, but how could he get around this? Salm was already with the lambs. At the doorway, Beri had taken over the table for customers to pay for their purchases. That spot was near enough to where Willow stood, putting one in a brilliant position to sneak in a question when she was between customers and Gran wasn't looking.

Maybe I can still make this work! Raven rapped Beri's shoulder. "Let me have my turn at this first."

Beri crossed his arms and glared. "Nay."

This was...rude. Raven huffed. "What's with you? Did you nae beat Salm to the center of the maze?"

Straightening, Beri glanced at Lady Lark helping two ladies with woolens inside the tent. "I have this job in hand. You help show the lambs."

Of all the... Blast it! He couldn't force Beri out. Frowning, he snapped, "You're to have a turn with them, too," before pivoting and striding over to join Salm in the sheep pen.

Beri slumped into the seat. If only this table were in the back of the tent. However, Ms. Scallop had it positioned at the doorway and instructed him to act as both host and sentry: greet the customers with a smile, offer his help, but don't let them leave without paying. That and the human note and coin exchange were his main duties, and since his parents had trained him as a child to handle their money, he knew it as well as Windborne trade credit.

Ms. Scallop had placed the cashbox—with Lark's peregrinator secured inside—in her tote bag in a crate under the table. With a knowing look, she'd said, "Keep your hand on the cashbox when you make a sale and return it here immediately. With a large lad like you in this chair, no one will attempt to snoop in our things. Do you ken my security measures?"

Aye, he did. And until someone was ready to impress them upon Raven, Beri wasn't budging.

Two little boys ran up to the lamb pen, followed closely by their parents. The family was dressed in everyday human shorts and shirts, looking like the families he remembered seeing long ago. Salm showed the boys how to hold their hands still so the curious lambs could sniff them.

A horn honked. Beri jumped. The boys didn't even look around, and he was envious of them. Their family was together and, at least here, away from human dangers. His parents hadn't been as fortunate.

He raked his fingers through his hair. He couldn't stop thinking of his mum.

Salm held back the lambs, while Raven opened the pen and allowed the family inside to pet the animals.

Beri stared up the line of crafter tents toward the manor house and the visitor car park in the field behind it, judging the distance. It was far enough away, and trees lining the drive to the house also stood in the way. He plucked up a pencil and drew hedgehogs on the paper for figuring sales, trying to concentrate on that rather than the automobiles. He'd seen the human vehicles a few times before today. Once, when they had gone to a human city as a family, he, his mum and his da. He'd been a wee lad, approaching fourth year. It was his second-earliest memory. The very earliest had happened the week before, when his da asked him to stop using magic to fetch every single thing he wanted.

"I can do it if we can go to a zoo," he remembered saying. He'd learned of them in a picture book and wanted to see the strange animals for himself.

Da had laughed. "You have to keep your magic locked away to go to a zoo, for only humans keep them."

Beri asked how, and over the morning, he learned to put away his magic in his storage cores. He didn't use magic the whole afternoon, not even when he played with his friends on the enclave's playground. He did everything "the human way" throughout the evening, setting the table, putting away his toys, selecting his books.

"I have a bedtime cookie for you." Da stood in the doorway and held out the plate. Beri remembered getting out of bed and walking over to collect it, something he never would have done before. His da picked him up and tossed him into the air, cheering that he'd passed a test.

In bed, he asked his mum, "Was I human enough to go to a zoo?"

Her long red hair fell across his cheek as she bent to kiss him good night. He caught it and, looking up into her green eyes, begged, "Please?"

They had gone to a zoo, and he loved it. He'd wanted to go

again and again, to see as many different kinds of animals as possible. Beri grimaced at that long-ago childhood wish. After his mum had died, they never did. Da had offered, but he'd been too afraid he'd lose him, too.

And then Da did die, in a completely different way, by cancer.

One of the ladies in the tent had selected a scarf to buy and placed it on Beri's table while she dug in her handbag.

"Pretty color," he murmured while he wrapped it the old-fashioned way Ms. Scallop liked, with brown paper and twine leftover from her hay bales. He took her money, brought the cashbox up onto his knees and gave her the change. "Have fun at the faire." He kept his hand on the box until she turned and then put it away.

He'd like to think this money exchange counted as *him* making a purchase for the trial, but he knew the others would call him on it. When the ladies left, Lady Lark came up beside him.

"Why don't you take a turn with the lambs? That was a fine start, but I know you, my lad. You'd rather have a conversation about animals. Salm can fill in here. I'll give him the cashbox instructions."

Beri did nae wish to test an argument with Lady Lark, so he made the switch when the family left. He settled down with the lamb that he'd held on his lap during the wagon ride here. Another family remarked on how tame the lamb was and came inside with their three children.

The boy, about ninth year, knelt beside him. "May I pet him?"

"Aye. His back is dandy, but expect a bit of a test nibble if you pet his face."

The lad offered his fingers up immediately to the lamb's teeth. He giggled when the lamb grazed them.

"Rory!" admonished his mum. "Did you nae listen?"

"I did! I wanted to see if it'd hurt."

"Brave lad you are," Beri said, and the boy beamed until he added, "However, the rest of us would like to see you safe. Let's stick to petting his back to keep the lamb calm. The tiny fingers of your wee sisters canna be tested."

Thankfully, the boy did, though he grumbled about his sisters stopping his fun.

"Feel around his ears for his horn nubs," Beri suggested. "Count how many you find."

Since the brown fleece wasn't long enough to really hide them, Rory quickly found all six. His parents were more interested in the Manx breed details Ms. Scallop had shared, and two blokes outside the pen asked how many the other lambs had. Beri nearly missed Rory teasing his fingers to the lamb's mouth again.

"Hey, I have an idea," Beri said brightly. "Find him a clover to eat."

Rory latched on to the suggestion, while his father helped the toddler lasses stroke the lamb's back. Beri let Rory feed his clover to the lamb on the flat of his hand, and the lad was thrilled.

"Brilliant distraction," Rory's mum said while her son crawled around to find more clover. "You must have younger siblings."

The suggestion caught Beri broadside, especially today, and he didn't know how to answer. Or if he *could* answer with his eyes pricking.

"Just me," Raven said from the pen's gate. "Hate to admit it, but Beri has hauled me out of trouble more times than I can count."

That got a cheerful response of, "We can't wait for Rory to be the girls' protector." Which Raven also answered.

Beri looked off, regaining his calm. After a moment, he noticed the blokes with the questions had retreated across the crafters' corridor, but were still staring at the lamb pen while talking. One elbowed the other, said something, and they walked away. Nothing in particular stood out about the men, in their twenties, or their gray shirts and denim trousers, quite unlike the green-skinned man sporting the flared, mushroom-like tubes from earlier who now approached their pen.

"Thank you," Beri mouthed to Raven.

The family was also thanking him and saying goodbye as they switched places with the burly, green-skinned man.

"Is my baby too young to pet the lambs?" he asked. While the baby scrunched his chubby fingers into the lamb's wool, Beri learned the man was play-acting an ogre from a movie that he didn't dare admit he'd never heard of.

So many people here were pretending, just like they were.

During a break in customers, Raven edged over to where Salm was chatting up Willow again. Lady Lark came from the tent to stand outside the pen next to Beri.

"You were right," he admitted. "It's easier to talk to folks with the lambs for conversation."

Lady Lark sighed. "Could you trust Merlin and me that this experience is meant for you to build trust in yourself?"

Spells, it was just like her to take one positive conversation and say the rest of the day would go as well. But... Beri glanced up at Lady Lark's earnest face. "I will try." It would make a good excuse when he used Oy's plan to duck out after speeding through the trial tasks.

Oyster and Coral returned with Ms. Scallop, followed by more families to see the lambs. Three of them managed the pen, while the other three helped with sales and wrapping. Beri met Merlin's gaze at one point, and he smiled. Surely this number of conversations with humans fulfilled one task on their list.

"Hear ye, hear ye!" shouted someone.

Beri lifted his head along with everyone else toward a fellow in a bright yellow and red, blousing outfit. His matching hood hung with something like stuffed horns, and he strummed an instrument as he stood on a small platform.

"Fair visitors to Cairnkin Village, come one, come all, and bear witness to our great tournament. Lords, knights and squires are suited up and ready to enter the field for a joust competition. The lances are measured, the shields deemed sturdy and their mounts lively. This hour, these brave knights match their skills for the prize of a gold circlet to be awarded by our royal court. Come assured of safe conduct by all!"

As he finished, people cheered and began filing away to the lawn area.

"Time for the lambs to take a break." Merlin threw the blanket across the corner to re-create their hide. "And for you young people to mingle and enjoy this event."

Beri rose and herded his lamb toward the shelter, as did Salm. Outside the pen, the others gathered around Merlin, but Beri busied himself moving the water bucket and hay for the animals.

"Beri?" Merlin jerked his bearded chin pointedly.

"Aye," he muttered. He'd told Lady Lark he would try. Time to put Oyster's advice into action. He came alongside Merlin and said, "Please tell me we've passed conversations."

Merlin seemed to sigh, but dipped his head down among them. Everyone leaned in. "Aye, I'll pass everyone on conversation. Excellent job this morning. Still to tick off are purchases and initiating conversations."

"How many purchases?" Beri asked. The doughnuts counted as one.

"I could buy something from every food stall," Coral declared.

Salm laughed. "I'm blimey grateful you don't have the money."

"Lunch, snacks and a half-dozen chats should be good," Merlin answered. "Go on now."

Salm took Coral by the arm and turned her toward a clump of people. "After the joust," he said. "I dinnae want to miss this."

While the others murmured their agreement, Beri scanned the route to the lawn area. People crammed the few openings between the trees, their excitement clear. The lines for food had all but disappeared. He eyed Coral, with her endless hunger. If he played this right, he could be back at the tent in a few minutes and avoid the dangerous crowding of people at that joust.

———

Once again, Raven ground his teeth when Salm maneuvered himself next to Willow. On her other side, Coral complained loudly that her brother was not the boss of her. Salm seemed oblivious to everyone...except Willow.

Then he caught Raven's eye and smiled.

The bloody git. "He knows he's taking my place," Raven growled to Beri.

"In a matter of days, Salm of the Seas will be off on their schooner, and you will have Willow to yourself for a week. Plot your way into her heart then."

"But if she encourages him—"

"Dinnae worry," Beri said distractedly.

"Cider to drink during the joust!" announced a woman from a booth. "Fresh apple cider."

"Doesn't that sound good?" said Willow.

This was his chance to get her something. Raven dug in his pocket for his money—

"Oh, I could use a drink," Coral said. "Please, let's stop!" She veered toward the booth, causing everyone to follow, with Beri now in the lead.

He planted himself before the server. "I'll pay for six of these." Beri waved to the cups. "One for each of us."

No, how could he ruin—

"As you wish, sir!" the costumed lady answered jovially. "Six pounds."

That much? Ho, he would never... But Beri scooped his human coins from his pocket, counted out the amount, and handed over a third of his money.

"Thank you," Willow said. "You must allow us to pay for lunch food for you."

Raven frowned. Beri must be up to something. He was kind, but this went beyond. Beri picked up a cup and turned, their gazes meeting.

Beri averted his and gestured for the others to collect theirs. "I'm not worried, because I know you'll remember to tell Merlin I have made this purchase."

As the others thanked Beri, Raven continued eyeing him. Beri attempted to arch his brows and look haughty, but red hair and freckles never came off as high and mighty. Aye, he was up to something.

Coral took a long drink from hers. "Mmm. Thank you so much! My throat was dry from all this talking."

Beri rolled his eyes. "'Tis nae over yet." He turned back to the server. "Where would you suggest standing to watch the joust?"

The woman brightened. "Even better, I can tell you how to avoid these crowds."

"Please do." Beri sounded relieved.

She directed them to go to the end of the crafter area before taking a narrower path through the trees. "Few people know it's there," she finished. "Circle around and look for a place along the rope. All spots are fair at the faire." She laughed at her pun.

Beri frowned. "Then we are nae avoiding the crowds *there*, only getting to them?"

She looked perplexed. "It *is* our most popular event. May your favorite knight win today!"

Jaw set in that way Raven knew to avoid, Beri scanned the clumped people and the distant path, then strode off in its direction.

Raven tossed a quick thanks to the woman and met Willow's gaze. She grimaced, and he probably did the same. At home, they'd let Beri go off and be grumpy by himself.

"Come along now, mates," Salm said cheerily and gave Willow a nudge to fall into step with him.

Nooo! Salm of the Seas would not get ahead with Willow, even if Raven had to punch him like a human to keep him back.

5

A CHIVALROUS RIVALRY

Raven hustled to stay right behind Willow and Salm as they threaded through the humans. Then he remembered Coral and Oyster behind him and peeked—they were there—and when he looked back, Salm was gone.

Where—

"Nay!" Salm's shout echoed as he pulled Beri back from a sandwich booth. "We are seeing the joust. *Come on.*"

Beri wrangled free to purchase a cookie and ask directions *again*. Salm herded the lot of them forward, then trekked ahead and took point, Coral and Oyster hurrying in his wake.

Grinning, Raven took Salm's place next to Willow. Beri lagged a half step behind, clearly irritated about something. He wasn't usually this stubborn, but if it distracted Salm, Raven was all for it.

They reached the hidden path in the trees and followed it to the expansive front lawn. Around the ropes, excitement built in the air like a wave of energy. People were bunched together three or more deep and standing on tiptoes. Raven had a decent view over their heads. However, beside him, Willow craned to see.

"Come along," Raven told her and clasped her elbow. A pleased feeling enveloped him for the minute they pushed together through the crowd after Salm.

"There won't be any horses running all the way down here," Coral complained.

Salm backtracked and grabbed the short lass' hand. "You're the one who wanted to stop for food," he reminded her. "I guarantee we will see this."

Ha. Coral's distraction allowed Beri to retake the lead, the others between and Raven and Willow bringing up the rear. More than fifty meters on, they could see the rope. Beri stepped up and turned to the last person along it. The man shook his head, like he was answering.

Willow nudged Raven's arm. "Did he ask that person a question, too?"

"Aye," he whispered. "Though he hates it, Beri will do what he's supposed to."

Beri waved them forward.

Coral reached him first. "What did you say to them?" she hissed.

"Anyone using this space?" he answered once they'd clustered around. "And they said…no!" He wrinkled his nose. "Aside from buying my lunch, I'm done."

Coral put one hand to her hip and shook a finger at him. "You have to buy…oh."

He gave her a smug look. "*The rest of you* have to buy snacks."

Raven huffed. "I tried, but you—"

"Look. The horses are coming," said Willow, sounding just like she did when diverting her little brothers from an argument.

Feeling his face heat, Raven turned his back on Beri and his completed tasks. Spells, with only the conversations completed, Raven was as far from the end of his trial as he was from speaking with Willow. He squelched a huff and shoved his tingling fingers into his pockets. He had to find a way to be alone with her again.

As Salm had promised, the riders paraded the length of the lawn, and each was introduced. Their names were long, and each began with Sir So-and-So, Knight from Wherever. Each listed an impressive number of jousts won—how was that possible?—or ladies in distress rescued and, one, a dragon slain.

Raven looked around at the others, trying to assess if they believed this rubbish.

Oyster whispered, "They are pretending here, too, are they not?"

"Aye," came several whispered agreements.

Ah. The announcer described their armor, as well as the types of training and games the real medieval knights would have done to prepare for battle.

"Good thing we escaped this world before all that happened," Salm said.

"The outfits are brilliant, though," Oyster said.

"Why are there no women riding as knights?" Coral asked.

Salm pointed. "The *chap* in blue? That's a lass."

Raven clapped him on the back. "Only you could pick that out, Salm, my good man."

"That's who I'm rooting for, then!" Coral called at the same time Oyster breathed, "Too bad. He was the cutest."

"The one in yellow is nearly as cute," Willow told him.

What? Raven studied the bloke. What was it Willow liked about him? Below his face shield, the chap had a neat goatee, which Raven was too young to grow. Neither would he be able to ride a horse or dress like that. Raven scowled. Sword skills, he might be able to manage if he trained...except he didn't know anyone who fenced. He turned to Beri to comment on the futility of matching this bloke, but Beri was staring out across the lawn, arms crossed.

Raven nudged him. "You have no reason to grumble when you've nearly finished."

Beri didn't even glance at him.

The riders returned to the far end. While the horses pawed and pranced, young squires ran out with cabbages under each arm. They set the leafy rounds upon the central wooden barriers and ducked away. A horn sounded. At a full gallop, the knights rode past, swinging swords and slicing through the cabbages.

After several rounds of that, and more of collecting rings onto the ends of lances, they began running at each other with padded poles, attempting to knock one another off their mounts. Coral's blue rider was eliminated. "She's not nearly as good at dodging as I am," Coral muttered.

Salm flicked one of his sister's braids good-naturedly. "Maybe she's not practicing as often. Or, I ken, she doesn't have as brilliant of an instructor!"

"Ha! You wish you could take the credit. But I'm that good. You'll see when I beat you."

"*If* you beat me, you mean."

"You've got a riding competition like this?" Willow asked. "Someplace you go on the mainland?"

The siblings stared at each other. "No, not exactly…" Coral pulled at one braid, suddenly becoming busy removing the tie and rebraiding it.

"'Tis a, uh, sailing thing we do." Salm gestured vaguely.

"Right, sailing," Coral echoed with too much cheer.

Salm gave a firm nod. "Trying to knock each other off the bow."

"Hey, Salm? I'm hungry," Coral said. "Come with me to get food."

He didn't want to, and after they argued a bit, Beri volunteered to go with her.

"Where will you go?" Raven asked. Beri scowled at him, and

Raven raised his hands. "Fine, no need to know." Sheesh, Beri was worked up.

"Doesn't matter," Salm said lightheartedly. "We'll wait right here until you return."

Beri and Coral left, and the jousts continued. The competitions were better than Raven had expected, and he found himself rooting for the yellow knight despite Willow favoring him. Or maybe because of her interest? These things were becoming confusing.

After another round ended, the crowd's clapping became excited calls as each knight moved his banner and a large bag to form a broad circle in the field. Along the rope, other youths leaned over to wave their hands and shout, "Pick me! Pick me!"

"What do they want to do?" Raven asked.

With a grin, Salm threw up his hand. "Who cares!"

The squires marched into the banner circle carrying armloads of foam and wooden weapons like they'd seen the children using earlier. To the cheers of the crowd, they dumped them into a pile and, with waves, came to stand facing their clamoring audience.

"'Tis time for the faire's volunteer squire challenge," the announcer boomed over his loudspeaker. "Sorry, you younger squires, but today's volunteers must be age thirteen or older!"

The knights rode on their horses up and down the barrier, hands to their brows and making a show of looking over the calling youth. The blue knight approached.

"Coral, your fav—oh." Salm looked around. "She's not back yet." He shrugged and waved his hand at the knight. When she looked at him, Salm executed his fancy bow again.

"Oh, really?" Raven scoffed. "You think that will work?"

The knight stopped, a broad smile on her face, and reached down to tap Salm's hand. "Who do I have the pleasure of training today?"

"Salm, at your service, Lady Knight!" He made another bow.

She laughed and tossed him a blue tunic, which Salm caught with one hand. "That's Sir Sarah, Blue Knight and Slayer of the Terrible Toothed Dragon. Come along, squire!"

Giving a cocky grin to the rest of them, Salm looked at Willow and said, "I'll make you proud," and then followed the knight onto the field.

Willow leaned toward the rope, intently watching Salm join a half-dozen other youths in the field.

Orb take it! Salm couldn't be doing better to impress her if he'd planned it.

"What about you, young man?" asked a man from behind Raven. "Fancy a friendly competition with your friend there?"

Raven looked up at the horse that'd approached and met the gaze of a knight in red. Several of the surrounding humans were pushing each other and the rope to get closer, but the knight was looking at him.

"Me?" Curses, he sounded like a git.

"I need a squire who can light a toasty fire. Has your training made you the lad to help me best Sir Sarah, the Blue Knight?"

He could light a fire. Raven glanced at Willow, wide-eyed at his shoulder. She looked scared. He shouldn't. They weren't supposed to draw attention, and some task might make him slip up. But if he could best Salm...

Oyster loomed into Raven's face. "Do it, lad. Prove yourself." He turned Raven by the shoulders to face the knight.

Raven raised a hand. "Yes, Sir..."

"Sir Richard, the Red Protector of the Righteous." He tossed a red tunic to Raven.

On the field, Salm did not look pleased as Raven strode out. "You have left Willow and Oyster alone," he hissed. "Coral and Beri are not back."

Raven put up two fingers, and Salm huffed. *What sorry excuse is that? He canna have forgotten we can go off in twos. Besides, Salm of the Seas couldn't boss him around.*

The other volunteers had arrived, and they donned the livery colors of the knight they served. Salm and Raven copied them, pulling on their tunics. The knights dismounted, and while the real squires led their horses away, they came to stand at their banners.

The crier with the funny hat and instrument had arrived with his crate and climbed on top of it again. "Faire visitors, you have seen the skill of our good knights," he announced. "We assume you feel your safety is guaranteed now. Yet always, we must look to our new ranks. Squires train from a young age to care for and later use the weapons of a knight. In medieval times, youngsters competed to be selected as a squire, for this was an apprenticeship that reflected on the knight's good training, as much as the squire. The winner of the last round has the honor of teaching the basics to this morning's potential squires."

Sir Richard, the Red Knight, came forward with his real squire and took the microphone. "A squire must be dressed in their knight's colors." He nodded to the volunteers. "Well done. Next, a squire is always armed. *Always.*"

The crowd laughed.

What was funny about this?

The Red Knight's squire put down the canvas bag she carried and began pulling things from it.

"You will find your belt and scabbard and put them on." The girl did so. "Sheath your sword. Adjust your shield brace and slide your arm into it." The squire did these things as well. It didn't look too hard, since everything was in the bag.

"Next, squires, set about your tasks. It was the duty of the squire to clean, pack and transport the knight's weapons. As was done in the days of old, today's squires must sort through the weapons to retrieve their knight's belongings, as identified by their colors. You're looking for eight items each."

Ah, he meant from the pile in the center. That didn't look difficult either.

"The squire must clean the mud from them and transport them to the knight's camp." He gestured to the circle of colorful banners. "Once at your camp, the squire must build and light a small—I repeat, small!—fire within the knight's brazier to warm their return."

"Squires! Are you ready?" called the crier.

The volunteers cheered along with the crowd.

"To your camps to await the signal to begin!"

Along with the others, Salm and Raven trotted to their knight's banner. Raven peeked at Willow—she was watching him! Then her gaze darted toward Salm, before coming back to him again. Time to do something to make sure she kept her gaze on him. The bag of weapons to wear lay at the base of his red banner, next to a box containing the metal pan and sticks of firewood. The weapons to gather were in the middle. Raven glanced toward Salm to see if he was doing anything different. Salm was eyeing two of the real squires approaching the equipment.

"Ladies and gentlemen! Squires in training," said the crier. "Remember these are weapons dirtied by the rigors of battle." The crowd began hooting when the squires held up packages and ripped their paper coverings. A white powder began pouring out, and they shook flour over all the weapons. Other squires approached with buckets, and Raven pinched his eyes shut. *Not honey, please!* It was water, so not as bad. Lastly, two squires trotted out with a canvas between them and flipped it over the lot. Bits of straw rained down on the sodden mess.

"The weapons must be cleaned," the announcer said. "The squire's tunic should remain respectably clean. And don't forget, you must always remain armed." Beside him, the red squire held up her arm with a shield on it.

They had to clean while wearing a shield? Blast, what had Salm gotten him into?

A whistle blew, starting the competition.

6

UPENDED PLANS

Why did I let myself get drawn into this? Raven struggled to buckle the costume belt and scabbard over his own belt. A plan hit him. He reached under the red tunic, unbuckled his belt and strung it through the shield's arm bands. He had to wear the shield, but not on his arm. He looped it across his chest, letting the shield hang on his back. A minute later, he wore the scabbard and sheathed plastic sword at his side.

One small, foot-square rag had fallen out of Raven's canvas bag when he'd upended it. He snatched it up and ran for the pile of weapons. Several others were there already, working one-handed and blocking others with their shielded arm as they wiped vigorously at weapon handles. He frowned. Eight pieces. Would they be all different?

Another kid ran up beside him, paused to scan the pile, then bungled his way into it, scattering the long pieces with kicking feet. "My jeans don't have to stay clean!" the boy crowed as he reached—and slipped. He landed with a thud on his rear on the flour-and-water-slicked ground.

A real squire ran over to give him a telling off about safety, and Raven moved several yards around the pile, only to come face-to-face with Salm.

He held dirty weapons in each hand, the shield on his arm like the others. His face lit with recognition upon seeing Raven, but the quip Salm must have had ready froze as his gaze landed on Raven's back and the shield there. "Ahoy, mate! Well done!"

Salm was complimenting him? "Thanks," Raven said automatically as Salm rushed off.

He reached into the pile and picked out a realistic-looking but lightweight mace, a sword, a lance and a dagger. That was four. No one had said he had to clean them here. He held two of the hay-flecked and oozy white weapons in each hand, gingerly away from his tunic, and minced out of the mud.

"Hey, that's mine!" A lass in a green tunic blocked his way, pointing to the mace.

Raven froze. What was he supposed to do? He couldn't get in an argument with a human. "I, uh, got it fairly," he muttered as he edged sideways.

"That one's green, you ken? It's mine." She slapped her belly —no, she meant the green tunic she wore.

Oh right, the mace handle was green. They were supposed to collect weapons only in their own color. He'd forgotten that among the other rules. Blast it. Were any of these red? He dropped the weapons between them. The lass grabbed her mace and swiped her flour-doughy fingers over others to expose their colors. An especially floured handle was red, so he grabbed it back.

She pivoted toward the pile, and he followed, carrying a dagger. No point in returning to his banner empty-handed. He searched among the weapons for the handles and swiped at the ones that weren't already clear of goo.

"Raven!"

His head popped up at Gran's shout filtering through the crowd's cheers. He found her at the rope, waving with Willow and Oyster. He waved back. Nice that Gran would be here to cheer him, but if he didn't find—

"Raven! Come here!"

This time, he straightened and really looked. Gran was upset. He started for her, but they were all waving and pointing at something else, so he stopped.

"Hey, you," yelled a lad elbowing past him. "Move if ye aren't going to pick any up. The rest of us need to get our stuff."

"Sorry." Raven trotted toward Gran and finally made out their calls of, "Get Salm!" He spun around, searching. Blue, blue... Salm was on the far side of the circle, crouched at his banner. Raven raced around. Whatever was going on must be bad. Though...not bad enough to use magic? Raven got within range and yelled, "Salm!"

His head lifted. Salm frowned.

"We've got to go. Gran is calling us over." Raven gestured to the crowd, only then noticing he still carried the dagger. He lowered his hand.

Shaking his head, Salm didn't even look. "Come now, that is a lame attempt to lure me away. You're even jeopardizing second place for yourself."

"Exactly!" Raven cuffed his shoulder. "I wouldn't! This is some sort of emergency." When Salm continued to wipe his weapons, Raven left, tossing out, "Look, would you?"

He ran from the circle, headed for... Only Willow and Oy were at the rope now. Where had Gran gone?"

"You there. Stop!" shouted one of the knights—his!

He stopped. Around the circle, the closest volunteer squires paused to stare at the man in red armor striding over.

How stupid I must look. "I have to go. Emergency with my gran."

"What? You got a call on your mobile? Or did you see you were too far behind?"

Raven searched again for Gran. Folks along the fencing yelled and pointed. His face heated. He didn't know what the bloke was talking about, and he didn't know the proper way to get out of this human competition, but he couldn't stick around to find out.

Salm trotted up, the scabbard banging against his leg. "Ahoy, Raven. Problem?"

His nerves loosened a bit. "We have an emergency, and he doesn't want to let us leave," Raven repeated slowly, as if explaining the situation to Willow's younger brothers. He tried to will Salm to understand he needed help here. That this wasn't a time to joke.

Salm moved in with him, shoulder to shoulder. "No problem with *volunteers* leaving, right?"

The knight frowned. "Give back the equipment, lads." He put out his hand.

That's all they had to do?

Raven handed over the dagger. Quickly, his fingers undid the buckles. The belts dropped, and he yanked the tunic over his head. He gathered the squire things to hand them back, but the knight was already reaching for Salm's and couldn't hold everything. Raven set his down. "Uh, bye." He spun toward Willow, Oyster and the booing crowd.

Salm joined him within steps, and they ran together.

"Glad you came," Raven said.

"Couldn't not do it, but hoy, I'd gotten the hang of the game. I was ahead!"

Oyster held up the rope for them, and they ducked under. Willow grabbed Raven's hand and pulled him with her, threading her way to the back of the crowd and toward the crafter area. Her warm fingers calmed him some, and he wished he had more time to enjoy their hands together and that she'd reached for him, not Salm. *Where is Gran?*

Willow stopped apart from the humans, who'd already forgotten about them, and the four of them clustered together.

"The cashbox was stolen," Willow said. "With a necklace of Lady Lark's inside it."

By the Orb! Raven pressed a hand to his forehead.

"She said..." Willow swallowed. "She said they both stepped inside to bring the rest of the scarves outside so a customer could see them in the daylight. When they came out, the man was gone, with the cashbox. Ms. Scallop went to report the theft, and Lady Lark came to fetch us to search with Merlin and Mr. Grouse."

"Then no one is watching the tent?" Salm asked. "That seems a tad risky."

"Nothing..." Raven took a breath. "Nothing is as important as getting that cashbox back." He scanned the crowd they'd left, the path to crafter area, the tents beyond. Where did they search, and for whom?

Oyster clasped his shoulder. "Her desperation... The way she said it and told us to tell you... 'Tis special in some way?"

Glumly, he nodded and spread his thumb and forefinger to the size of a peregrinator's glass rod and placed them at his sternum where one would hang.

The other three's mouths dropped open.

"We must get it back. Otherwise, Gran is..." He couldn't think about what might happen to her. He began trotting toward their tent, the others falling into step with him. "And Beri left with Gran to help?" he asked Willow.

"No," she cried. "He and Coral never came back!"

7

RIGHT PLACE FOR THE WRONG REASON

As Beri walked through the woods, alone and among familiar flowers, trees and shrubs, the weight of dealing with the faire dropped from his shoulders. Even the calls of the birds were mostly the same as on the isle, and the deer had nibbled twigs of their favored shrubs. The best thing, thank the Orb, was no crowd. Here, the sounds of nature swept the estate's hum to the background, and he had no fear of the automobiles while he was among the tree trunks.

Though muffled, the traffic noise still reached him. Could humans never escape it? This only proved that the human world was not the place for him. That was a difference in the wizard versus human lives to relay to Merlin: Wizards lived more quietly.

He had to shake the fear that made his skin crawl and steel himself for the rest of this endless day. Emptying his mind of what was yet to come, he breathed the scent of soil and decomposing leaves.

Ahead grew a good-sized oak with many lower limbs, and it was nothing to grip the rough bark and pull himself up into it.

His back to the trunk—and the faire—he settled in with a view of birds flying about the trees.

Raven broke into his thoughts, and Beri's first reaction was to brush him off. Ach, Raven was going to get them in trouble again. He shouldn't answer... Then Raven's question sank in: *Where are you and Coral?*

I am... What do you mean? Isn't Coral with you and the group?

No, and neither are you.

Merlin's orders of *stay together* echoed in his head. *I watched until she rejoined the group. I...needed time alone.* It was one thing for him to be alone among the trees. The woods were safe. But a fourteenth-year lass alone in this crowd with no magic...

Beri rose to stand on the limb. *This communication is against the rules—*

Don't you think I bloody well know it? Raven shouted in his head. *We have a blasted problem. Coral is missing. The cashbox has been stolen. Gran's peregrinator has been stolen. I've gotten through to you, but Salm can't reach Coral. She must have shut down her channels.*

Beri clutched at the tree's rough trunk to steady himself. By the Orb, this was awful. They couldn't lose either Coral or the device. He crouched and jumped to a limb facing the house. As he did, a feeling of lightness came over him—oops, his...magic.

A quick look told him no one was watching the trees. And this might be a bloody emergency. Something the DMR wouldn't penalize the enclave for. Besides, the council wanted them trained to react in an emergency.

Gran needs our help, Raven sent. *Willow and I are on our way to find out what the man looked like. Oy and Salm are searching for Coral. They can thought-speak with each other, but otherwise, it's only siblings—you and I, and Salm and Coral. And we're not supposed to be doing it, so...*

We have to, Beri sent back. *We canna lose Coral. Plus, if that device gets lost, Lady Lark is in major trouble.* Even this far away from the jousting, its announcements carried. Crowds still lined the lawn.

If Coral had left the event, then this was the time to find her. She was a small lass, but easier to find than a metal box.

We're at the tent—ho! The lambs are loose. I only see one. Dad—

How did that happen?

An announcement was made at the jousting area, to many cheers. While Beri waited excruciating seconds for Raven to answer, light music started up, and the chatter swelled. Something was happening on the stage. If he waited much longer, the crowd would fan out, making it that much harder to spot Coral.

Beri scanned the people strolling, filtering through them as he did when searching the bushes for grouse…maybe with a touch of his usual magical method. Nae tall, nae bright clothes or dark, nae paired. Small, blue outfit, alone.

The purple-haired chap at the doughnut table. Might he remember her? If he worked for the estate, would he know how to search the grounds?

Dad says leave the lambs, Raven finally said. *We've got to find Coral and the cashbox.*

I'm searching the east side of the house where we bought the doughnuts—

"Ahoy, stop!" The shout cut through everything else, and Beri jerked his gaze beyond the maze's entrance. Coral's blue blouse and brown braids popped into view. Her back to him, she was running down the wide gravel roadway behind the manor house, dodging people.

Spells, there she is! Running like she's being chased.

What? Where?

Beri leaped from the tree, landing a good ways from the trunk. By the Orb, magic again! He couldn't, not in public. He ran. Out of the woods and across the first bit of lawn that was clear. Ahead, people strolled along, unaware.

Beri, be more specific!

*Maze entrance. Behind the house and headed toward the main gate and—*he swallowed—*the car park.*

8

A TEST OF CONFIDENCE

Beri's head clouded with the weight of finding Coral again. He might be the only one to have spotted her. Would he be fast enough to catch up to her across the estate grounds?

You fetch her, Raven sent. *We're getting the thief's description from Gran.*

Beri sprinted over the grass. Music blared anew. Folks began to spread across the lawn area. Some queued up to enter the manor house, others swarmed the paths to return to the crafter area, while others came this way around the doughnut booth and headed toward the maze.

Gran says the bloke who disappeared with the cashbox is wearing a gray shirt, denim trousers and has brown hair.

The description prickled at Beri as familiar somehow, but why? As he entered the crowd, the passersby blended together, many wearing the overly fancy costuming common at the faire, but enough wore the plain shirts humans favored that a gray shirt wouldn't stand out. Beri darted around folks, craning looks ahead at the roadway Coral had been on. Searching for blue and braids... Blast, he'd lost his view, but that'd been Coral, he was sure.

Their wagon in the vendor car park and the crafter tents were to the left of that roadway. If she'd returned toward the crafter area, she'd run into the others and be fine. But if Coral had turned right, into the public car park... As much as he hated the idea, he had to trust that he could catch up and help her.

Trust what happens will be right. He hadn't thought of Da's words in years. He'd said them seven long years ago when they'd moved to the Isle of Giuthas, the Windborne island his da had grown up on. It was when Da found out about the cancer. He'd asked Merlin if he'd raise Beri. Merlin and Raven had been warm and welcoming and, with Lark, had folded him into their family as if he'd been their own blood kin. But to eighth-year Beri, knowing he was losing his da had been the end of his world.

Beri broke out of the crowd around the side of the doughnut tent. The roadway of gravel lay ahead between the maze hedges and the manor house. Fewer people were back there. Most were walking toward him, headed for the maze entrance.

"Hey! Beri!" called a shrill voice, and Rory, the boy from earlier with the lambs, ran up. Lengths behind him came his mum, trying to catch up. "I saw a man carrying your brown lamb in the car park," Rory panted. "I told him he shouldn't be doing that, but my mum said to be quiet."

"Rory, you aren't supposed to run ahead!" shouted his mother, still yards off. "We have to meet Dad, then we can report it."

"He was stolen!" Rory shouted. "It's an emergency!"

As Rory's mum hushed him, the purple-haired doughnut seller ran up. "You have an emergency?" He waved a radio device and looked between them.

Clearly, he was offering help, and while Beri couldn't explain outside of their group exactly why a *necklace* in a cashbox was an emergency, he could get help for Ms. Scallop's money. He'd be free to help Coral, then.

"Aye," Beri said. "He says he saw one of our lambs in the car park, but also our cashbox was stolen, and one of our lasses is missing, though I think I just saw her running that way, too." He turned to go, but the purple-haired lad thrust out a hand.

"Heard about a cashbox," he said. "That'll be hard to trace, but you've a missing child from your group? Description?"

"Youth—teen. Coral is fourteenth year." Ach, he'd said that wrong, but couldn't stand around explaining. Beri backed toward the car park. "Blue dress, brown braids. I have to find her."

"That girl is with the man carrying your rare lamb!" Rory yelled in exasperation.

"Oh." The doughnut seller's eyes widened with recognition. "You don't mean Ms. Meadows' lambs? The Manx ones?"

Rory thrust out a finger. "That's what I've been saying. Come on!" He sprinted back down the roadway.

His mum shouted, "Rory!" and started after him again.

Beri took off and passed her. Behind him, more footsteps pounded. The doughnut lad called, "Security Code A. Possible child abduction. A missing teen, blue dress and brown braids, last seen headed for the car park. One of the rare Manx lambs was also seen there. Search the car park and stop anyone with a young teen girl or sheep."

Beri had to smile. Rory had gotten attention and help in a way that Beri never could have. He hadn't known it was possible. Though his mother was yelling, she was behind them, too, and he wouldn't let Rory out of his sight either.

More folks were on the roadway ahead at the end of the hedges. No sign of Coral, yet he easily kept Rory in sight.

Then Rory turned right into a gap in the boxwood hedge. *No! Not the maze.* He had no sooner disappeared than Salm burst out of woods from the opposite side. Their gazes met. Beri pointed, but wide-eyed Salm had scanned between them and turned to search the other direction.

"Salm!" gasped Beri. Blast it, why couldn't it have been Raven, who he could thought-speak with? Salm clearly hadn't found Coral…unless he was now looking for the thief.

Salm began running the opposite direction, down the tree-lined corridor toward the main gate. Beri was almost to the turn Rory had taken. He had to forget Salm and go after the boy… and find Coral. But if Rory had gone into the maze, he might never find them.

We see you, Raven sent. *Behind you and coming. Where is she?*

He hoped it wasn't the car park. *Not sure, but I'm following a boy who says he saw her. Salm ran past.*

We'll find her.

Raven sounded so sure that Beri repeated, *Trust what happens will be right.* He reached the gap in the hedge. Ahead, Oyster came out from around the end of the manor house. He saw Beri and stopped.

Beri pointed. "Salm went that way. You didn't see Coral?"

Oyster shook his head. "Salm is frantic that someone has kidnapped her!"

"I'm not sure." Beri pointed again. "I'm following a boy who saw her over here." He ducked between the bushes where Rory had gone.

Oyster followed him. "I'll tell Salm through my channels. Let's go."

They ran. The path wasn't into the maze, thank the Orb. It skirted alongside the boxwood, with woods on the other side. He couldn't see Rory.

"Salm will circle around from where he is," Oyster whispered.

Movement ahead caught Beri's eye. Rory's figure became clearer in the thinning woods…aye, because this path opened to the field of automobiles. *Orb take it.* Beri's heart raced, far worse than it had from running. Some would be moving in this field.

His heartbeat kept pace with the pounding of footsteps. Would Rory—

"Rory! Watch out for the cars!"

The boy stopped, looking back, then forward again.

"Wait!" Beri shouted.

"But—" Rory dashed back. "The guy's there, fighting with the girl over the lamb."

"Let go!" snapped Coral, and Beri saw her a hundred feet ahead, a small blue-clothed figure tussling with a much bigger man in gray.

Gray shirts. *Two* men wearing gray shirts had asked them about the lambs. They had brown hair. Was one of them the cashbox thief, and the other had let out the lambs? And chased Coral? Or had Coral seen the man with the lamb, and *she'd* chased him?

I see you, Raven sent. *Where is Coral?*

"The missing lambs are over here?" asked Oyster.

This was getting crazy with too many people talking to him. Plus, Rory had sprinted ahead again. Beri kept running. At the end of the path, a few folks were bunched up around the gray-shirted man, who had one of their lambs draped around his neck and out of Coral's reach.

"Hey," someone shouted. "Why are you—"

"My sheep are my business," the man snapped.

"That's not your lamb," Coral yelled.

"It's not!" Rory added.

"Damned kids," snarled the man. "Get out of my way." He shoved past a couple, a man in a white shirt and a woman in green.

Flights! Coral was fine, but... "Stop him," Beri shouted as he and Oyster ran.

The woman saw them, whipped around to the thief and shouted, "Lamb-napper! You give her lamb back!"

"Coral is here," Oyster said, then a second later, "Salm sees us."

The man in white gave chase and grabbed the thief by the shirt. As the thief lurched, the lamb flew from his shoulders and landed on the ground with a bleat. Gray Shirt swung and punched the other man in the gut, while the lamb got to its feet and ran between the cars. White Shirt hit back and shoved the lamb-napper against a car. The woman screamed, and Rory yelled and hurtled after the lamb.

Beri winced. The cars were parked, yet… *I canna think of the danger. I must get Rory. He canna become a memory like Mum.*

Or—

"Coral!" he shouted as she chased after the lamb, too.

The fighters fell to the ground, rolling in the narrow corridor of grass between the cars. Beri leaped over them. He should help, but he couldn't lose sight of Rory or Coral.

No cars were moving in the car park—only Coral and Rory darting zigzags as the bleating lamb trotted around the side of this car then that one.

The animal wouldn't calm down until they stopped chasing it. "Leave…" The order died in his throat, because striding down the driving aisle came the second gray-shirted man. The man who had asked the questions at the pen. Their gazes met across a row of cars.

These men must also have their cashbox with Lark's peregrinator.

The man registered recognition a second before a yell from the fighters broke his stare. A moment later, the lamb ran from between the cars practically at the man's knees. He grabbed it—clearly experienced at this—and swung the lamb onto his shoulders and turned.

"Hey!" Rory yelled, Coral echoing him, "Put him down!"

Coral gave chase, but the boy was slower. Beri managed to grab Rory's shoulder.

"Nay. You stop and wait for—" He looked around. The boy's mum was nowhere in sight. Then Oyster careened around a car, the mum and doughnut fellow on his heels, thank the Orb, and Raven and Willow behind them.

"Rory," his mum shouted.

"You wait for your mum," Beri ordered and took off after Coral.

"Aw, I wanna help!" His wail mixed with pounding footsteps.

Beri raced after Coral.

An engine started up. Which was it? Fear squeezed Beri's gut as he frantically searched for the automobile—and spotted Salm across the car park.

He pointed, but at what? The car? Coral?

Oyster caught up to him as Raven asked, *You have a plan? I wish I still had that squire dagger. It looked real enough.*

A dagger? Spells, they didn't need weapons. *He might have the cashbox,* Beri answered and also said that aloud to Oyster. *Since they've taken the lambs.*

Ah, good thinking.

Oyster grunted his agreement.

They were nearing the end of the row where a white van was parked unevenly next to the other cars. A man in the driver's seat, clearly with the two crooks, leaned out of his window and yelled, "Hurry!"

Beri heard it now. The running engine was the van's. And he had to go near it to save the lamb and Coral.

"The white van," Oyster panted out. "You see it? Good. Salm is on it, too." He waved across the car park.

It was the oddest conversation...which wasn't completely directed at him. Beri narrowed his focus to stopping the man. Coral was already yanking his shirt, and now he and Oyster had Raven and Willow to help. He had to trust all of them.

The man rounded the van with the lamb, Coral beside him.

Beri skirted the back, close enough his shoulder rubbed the

metal side. Its vibrations coursed through his body. He sucked in a breath, and sweat beaded on his brow.

Nay, naught was stopping him! He plowed forward, around the van—

At a side opening, the thief shoved Coral off, but she nimbly leaped aside and made another grab for the lamb. Beri extended his arms and lunged into the man. His hold on the lamb faltered. It fell, and Coral tumbled after it, while Beri forced the thief backward, slamming them both against the open passenger door.

Right. Now what? Beri was chest to chest with the thief, a clean-shaven man sporting a neat haircut, looking no different than someone who might be on the deckways of Tern Bay. Except he'd robbed them. "Where's our cashbox?"

"What're we waiting for?" the driver shouted. "Get in!"

"Not with our lamb!" Coral yelled back and clambered through an open sliding door.

Hadn't the lamb run off? The thief shoved Beri back—or tried to. Oyster threw himself beside Beri's larger frame and pinned an arm. The man yelled at them, and the driver yelled at Coral, and Beri bent his knees and leaned into the bloke with all his muscle. They wouldn't last much longer. Where were Raven and Willow?

Over the man's shoulder, Beri saw Salm appear through the window. He sprinted around the door. "What the hell! No one kidnaps my sister!" He jabbed his fist, landing a neat punch on the man's jaw. He sank in Beri's hold. Beri let him fall, and as the thief attempted to get up, Oyster hit him, then sat on him. Willow plopped onto his feet.

Inside the van, Coral was frantically trying to untie another wide-eyed lamb tethered to a seat. "Stupid way to tie a knot!"

"Ho!" Beri shouted. "Unbuckle the collar!"

The van roared as it started forward. *Coral!* Beri leaped into the van, swaying with its movement but pushing on. Coral was undoing the collar, then the lamb was free and tried to scramble to the back. Beri shoved it toward the door, and the lamb jumped out. He grabbed Coral under the arms to pull her up.

On the floor lay their cashbox.

"By the Orb," he blurted. "Get it." He pointed.

Coral snatched up the box. He hauled her upright and swung around. The ground moved past the open door. *It'll only get worse.* They had to do it. "We're jumping!"

With the van accelerating, he lifted Coral and jumped. Magic flushed through him automatically, just as it would for flight, and his body lightened. Even bearing Coral's additional weight, the familiar feeling of floating came over him. They drifted, and he landed on his feet, running. The momentum carried them a few paces before he stopped and let Coral slide to the ground. She looked as breathless as he felt, and he ought to ask if she was all right, but he took the cashbox and flipped the latch.

Please, don't let it have been opened and the peregrinator discovered.

The coin tray was on top, the different coins jumbled together now, but that wasn't what mattered. He lifted the tray... The paper envelope was on the bottom, puffed with the wool padding. Seeing it wasn't enough to satisfy him. He handed back the box, opened the flap and felt around with his fingertips. The chain and glass rod were there. Relief made his knees wobble.

He closed the envelope and slid it into his pocket. He would nae let go of it until the device was again in Lady Lark's possession. Tilting back his head, Beri released his breath. A weight lifted from him. Back when he was eighth year, he was sure his Da dying would be a blasted horror that he'd never recover from.

He had. Or maybe he was still. It was hard to tell, but he was making a place for himself, with the help of his new family. Aye, Da had been right. Things were turning out right, and as Lark had said, this experience was for him to build trust in himself. He had, and everything had worked.

The purple-haired doughnut lad trotted up, breath heaving, radio to his mouth. "Car park. White van roaring out. Stop it! Kids are—" He whirled to Beri. "Are *all* of you here?"

A quick scan found Oyster, Willow *and* Raven on the thief, Salm hugging Coral, who was hugging their cashbox, and two lambs staring from between parked cars. "Aye!"

"Everyone is safe," the doughnut lad shouted into his device. "Get the number plate if you can't stop it. And some help over here!" Then he bent, hands to his thighs, and gasped in a few breaths. "I gotta lay off the doughnuts."

TRUST PAID OFF

Holding down the struggling thief took all of Raven's strength. Willow deftly pinned his kicking feet—how many times had he seen her do that to her younger brother? With the thief hurling constant profanities over his shoulder, Oy had the worst of it.

"You're in for more trouble than you bargained for," the man growled. "I'll track you down wherever you live!"

Raven looked at Willow and Oyster, and their gazes met. They burst out laughing.

A tremendous screech and bang erupted from the direction of the entrance gate, silencing them. While their thief quietly groaned, they craned to see what had happened. Jesters, knights and a number of uniformed guards ran down the adjacent roadway. At the doughnut lad's shout, several split off and ran over to help them.

The staff bound the thief's hands. One said, "We'll take over now, kids," and hauled the man upright. Only then did Raven notice the speaker was the Red Knight.

He paused when their gazes met. "This was your emergency?" asked the Red Knight.

Blast, was the man going to reprimand him again? Raven gestured helplessly. "They stole our cashbox and our rare lambs. We had to help our friends."

The knight laughed. "A far better way to prove you have earned the right to defend the kingdom. I shall see that you both receive your inductions." He lifted his chin toward Salm.

Er? "Right, thank you!" Raven said before an odd question slipped from his mouth.

Police sirens wailed over the confusion. The couple who'd fought one of the thieves approached with a uniformed guard leading the scoundrel, hands cuffed behind him and his head hanging. The boy Beri had called Rory and his mum trailed after them.

"You're all right?" Raven asked Willow, and at her nod, he extended a hand to Oyster. "You have a mean hook, mate." Raven never would have thought to punch these humans as Oyster and Salm had.

Oy shook his hand. "We all did well." His glance included Beri, Coral and Salm standing nearby.

They had, if only the cashbox…then Raven's heart leaped at spying the box in Coral's hands. *Beri? Is the—*

I have it. He patted his pocket.

Raven grinned broadly. *Thank the Orb.*

Willow elbowed his ribs. "'Tis a relief, isn't it?"

"Oh, ho! You have no idea." He put his arm around her shoulders and pointed to Coral. "They found Gran's per—*necklace!*" Willow leaned into him for a moment—long enough that Raven realized what he'd done—then she hugged him and let out a whoop of glee. They were apart again as quickly as it'd happened. Had she meant to? Confusion muddled his thinking, and his face blazed. Immediately, he turned to Oyster and whispered the news as they joined the other three.

"I wasn't kidnapped or lost," Coral was saying indignantly as she swatted Salm's arm. "'Twas *nae* Beri's fault. We got within sight of you all, and he said he had business to attend to. I know that means a trip to the loo, so I thought I had time to sneak off to get another doughnut. Before I could, I saw that bloke carrying away Ms. Scallop's lamb, the lighter one I'd held this morning with the braided leather collar. I *knew* it was hers. I'm sorry I scared everyone, but he wouldn't let her go, and I couldn't..."

Use magic to stop the man. Raven got that, but had following an unknown, maybe dangerous, human been worth it for a sheep?

She planted her fists on her hips. "I wasn't about to break the rules and figured he'd be no more of a problem to get something away from than Salm. But he was, and I was glad for the help," she finished with a defiant grin.

Raven grinned back. That was Coral, feisty in the face of danger. He extended his hand for her to shake. "You did what you could. We each did."

"Trust what happens will be right!" Beri practically cheered. "We wouldn't have found the cashbox if you hadn't kept after him. You and Rory spotted the thieves."

Speaking of... "Come on, mates," Raven said, "we should catch these lambs."

Between them, the lambs were easily corralled. Raven went to remove his belt to use as a leash and discovered he no longer wore it.

"Argh," he cried. "I left my belt at the joust."

Beri thumped him on the back and handed over his own belt, repeating, "Trust what happens will be right!"

Raven groaned. "Is that your new mantra?"

The doughnut lad approached them, his purple hair loose and wild about his face. "I'm Ian, and the estate security team wants you to tell them what happened. I'll get this lass that doughnut, and some for everyone, while you wait to tell the authorities your story." He spoke into his radio.

Oh. Raven glanced around, and the six of them moved closer like magnets. None of them looked assured about *their story*.

"What are we to do?" Oyster asked. Even Salm didn't have an answer. They'd drawn notice, maybe not by using magic, but neither had they *fit in*.

Ian finished on his radio. "Where are your parents?"

Salm tried to explain but not explain. Raven steeled himself to watch his tongue. They might have caught the thieves. However, this...this was dangerous and more than they should handle. "My dad is with us," Raven said. "Shall I fetch him?"

"I'll go with him," Willow announced. "We're from out of town, and after this, none of us should be alone." She slipped her hand into his.

Raven's fears evaporated. Willow was a quick thinker, and he was glad to have her by his side. He smiled at Willow and squeezed her fingers. Everything would be fine, even if their elders decided their actions meant they'd fail their trial.

Ian accompanied them, and another faire worker came along to stay and watch their tent.

As they approached, Gran's gaze found him. The tight creases at the corners of her frantic eyes were a sharp contrast to this morning's placid look. Raven released Willow and strode ahead to hug his grandmother.

"We found it," he whispered. "Beri has it safe."

"Thank the Blessed Orb!" she mumbled under her breath. She held him tight, and when they parted, she had to wipe her eyes on her apron.

On the return to the manor house, some furious thought-speaking was happening privately between Dad, Gran, Ms. Scallop and Mr. Grouse. With the adults following behind, and Ian leading them through the groups of chatty people, Raven was even more aware of being in step with Willow, her hand once more firmly in his. A bubble of quiet, like in a pereport, settled around them. Maybe this wasn't the best time, but it was probably as much privacy as they were likely to have, especially if they might have to leave the faire. He had to ask her now.

Raven leaned his head to hers. "Do you think," he started. No, that wasn't right. His hands were suddenly clammy. "Willow?" He started again. Why did he say her name when she was already looking at him? *Just say it!* "I really like you," he blurted. "More than friends. Would you be willing to prebond with me to see if—"

Her eyes twinkled yellow with her energy.

Oh Blessed Orb!

Willow dipped her head, and her blond hair fell like a curtain to hide her face.

What did that mean? He swallowed. He hadn't finished asking. "If you like me the same," he said at the same moment Ian turned and said, "Stick close!"

Raven clamped his lips shut. Had he seen? Heard?

Willow dropped his hand and pressed hers to her brow. Head down, she shoved on after Ian, who called, "Excuse me, folks! Faire business," and pushed through a gathered crowd.

Raven blew out a breath and kept pace with Willow. She wouldn't look at him. *No...*

This wasn't going well. Not at all.

Disappointment pricked at his energy, and only the fear of losing face in front of Willow was keeping it down. *Now she knows how I feel. She can bring it up later...*

But if she didn't... *Orb take it, what will I do?*

Ahead, Ian came to a rope blocking the roadway and the route to the manor house. He gestured urgently to a police officer holding back the onlookers. Beyond, other officers loaded the three handcuffed thieves into their official cars. More police circled the white van that had crashed into a hedgerow. Two staff members dressed as peasants to welcome visitors at the fancy gate stood proudly with their pitchforks—and two officers.

The Windborne adults bunched up behind them, while Ian

told the officer, "I need to use the side entrance to take the people who were robbed into the estate offices."

They were allowed through to walk down the roadway, and Raven could feel people staring at them. He groaned. Again, this was the exact opposite of blending in. Beri was going to have a fit when the elders failed them.

Ian ushered them into the quiet house and upstairs where the only evidence of the medieval festivities were the costumes on Ian and two other knights. Everyone who'd stayed with the police was gathered in a meeting room, Beri and the others from the isle, the couple who had helped and Rory's family. Officers were interviewing the adults.

While Dad and the other chaperones followed Ian to the officers, Gran clasped Raven's elbow and steered them toward Beri. She met Beri's gaze, and he gave a nod and tilted his head to his hand in his trouser pocket. Gran slid into the empty chair next to him, and Raven stood between them and the room. Willow stepped beside him, shoulder to shoulder, like it was a natural thing to do.

Would it be enough to block the view?

Without so much as a word—nor a thought-spoken message, by Raven's judgment—Beri slid his hand from his pocket. The puffy envelope was visible for a split second before Gran's hand wrapped around it and shoved it deep into her skirt pocket.

Her shoulders slumped, and for a moment, she leaned back and closed her eyes. Her lips moved, suspiciously like when she cast a spell. She looked sheepishly at them and whispered, "What I should have done in the first place—locked it to me."

Then she withdrew her hand and threw her arms around Beri. "Thank you so very much, lad," she said. "I want to hear more later, but for now, tell the others I am beyond grateful." She stood and hugged Willow and Raven, too.

He bent his head to her ear. "Will you tell the council?"

"Nay. We—Scallop, Merlin and Mr. Grouse—agreed if it was

recovered, we would take this as a lesson and never mention it again."

Beri had stood as well. "Ach, if the elders are nae in trouble, what about the youths? Have we drawn too much attention to pass our trials?"

Gran frowned. "We haven't had the time to discuss your actions. Be patient and carry on." Placing a finger to her lips, she turned and joined her cousin.

With a grunt, Beri plopped down. Raven lowered onto the adjacent chair, and Willow sat next to him. Beri passed them a box of doughnuts, and when Raven waved it off, Beri said grumpily, "Gives your mouth a reason not to be talking."

They each took one.

While Gran and Ms. Scallop spoke to one officer with a pen and clipboard, Dad stood by watching Mr. Grouse answer questions for another, listing them with names that must be more human. "Beri Moors, Raven Meadows, Coral and Salm Sea—ah, Seward." Mr. Grouse blinked rapidly.

Aye, they couldn't all have names coming from nature and fit into the human world. Ha! Something their elders had never considered. Down the row of seats, Coral mouthed the new name—blast, *he* better pay heed and also remember them.

The officer put up a hand. "Hold on! One at a time."

Mr. Grouse bobbed his head several times, and when he was directed to continue, he announced more firmly, "Oyster Ester-brook and Willow Ashton."

They told their stories, minus the magical conversations. They had to claim they ran into each other and ended up in the car park.

The officer lifted a finger. "Though your actions were heroic —and, fortunately, successful—chasing down those thieves was dangerous." He frowned at Coral. "For you in particular, young lady. Why were you separated from your brother and friends?"

Coral peeked at Salm, and he gave a slight nod. "I was sneaking off to buy a doughnut."

"I'm sure you both have heard this before," the officer said, sweeping his gaze over Rory, too, sitting nearby with his mum. "Children your age need to stay with your parents or older friends. No one should be wandering alone at a public event until you are at least a teenager. Thirteen."

"But-but I'm fourteenth—fourteen!" sputtered Coral.

The officer looked between her and Rory. They were about the same size.

"She is," said Salm, echoed by Mr. Grouse.

"Beg your pardon, miss." He stalked off to talk with another officer, then again called over their chaperones.

Coral grumbled to Salm, and beside Raven, Willow blew out her breath. Then she changed seats to sit next to Coral and put an arm around her.

Raven sank in his seat. Not a word, and now she wasn't even sitting next to him. This didn't look good for him. But as he watched Coral whispering to Willow and Willow whispering back, his bad humor lessened. More important things had happened today. They were still together. No one had slipped up and used magic.

Beri nudged him. "Trust what happens will be right. I did, and I was able to run among those automobiles to help Coral and find the cashbox. Your turn will come."

Raven scowled, just because it was easier than agreeing. "Can I remind you when it doesn't?"

Finally, the Windborne adults and Rory's dad returned with Ian and another man in a suit.

"They'll be pressing charges on our behalf," Dad said. "We're fortunate nothing of ours was lost."

The man in the suit cleared his throat. "Yes, yes. Thank you to everyone in this room. My staff can't be everywhere, so we extend our appreciation to each of you who saw something suspicious and spoke up. But as the director of the Cairnkin Manor Foundation, I must enforce our policies that incidents must be reported to us—as they were—and then the matter left for our *trained* security staff to act upon." He paused. "Do you understand that you put yourselves at risk?"

Ho, they were in trouble. Now their elders had the breaking of human policies to use against them passing as well. Raven nodded, along with everyone else.

"Right, then," the man said. "Next time—should there be one—everyone will follow procedure. I regret this has spoiled your day at the faire, so we have free passes for each of you to attend next year's faire. And today, would you do us the honor of joining the royal family for lunch in their grandstand box to view the midday joust?"

Coral squealed. She whirled to Merlin and clasped her hands. "Please? Please, please!"

Fifteen minutes later, after the faire staff had taken their orders for lunch to be brought to the joust, Ian and another knight escorted their group to the grandstand. They queued up to wait along the back of the building for their introductions, following the royalty, of course. Ian was showing off his ring collection to the girls and Oyster—but mostly Oyster—and Salm was talking up the Blue Knight while keeping his arm around Coral's shoulders. Raven was resigned to Willow sticking with Coral. Then she squeezed in beside him.

She'd come over on purpose, but didn't say anything. That could mean only one thing—to tell him *no*. Raven blew out a breath. He leaned down to whisper, "I get it. Salm's a lifelong friend, too, and a good fellow. I don't blame you for wanting to prebond with him and hope—"

Willow burst out laughing. "That is nae what I was about to say. I mean, aye, Salm is a nice friend and everything, but... You caught me by surprise earlier. My...*I* slipped and had to settle *things*."

Oh. *Now* he understood. Her magic had slipped. That's why she'd hidden her face and gone quiet.

"I would like to prebond with you," she said.

"You would?" His heart leaped. "I mean, you would. Brilliant!" He felt great...except for one thing. He shouldn't ask, but if not now, when it had been a large part of their day, then when? "So, what about Salm? He certainly looked like he wants to ask you the same."

Willow scrunched up her nose. "Salm is...Salm. Nae serious enough for me."

"But he's good at magic and following the rules, pleasing the elders..." *Orb take it, what am I doing, trying to convince her I'm a rotten choice?* He should shut his trap.

"You, Raven of the Meadows, don't give yourself enough credit for your efforts. You attempt these things as often as the rest of us, and even succeed as much as we do. You shouldn't compare yourself to others. I think you're perfect as yourself."

Right. Good. This was...good. "I think you are, too." He grinned like a git.

She did, too, for a moment, then sobered. "But we canna until we both turn sixteenth."

Well, yes, he'd known that, but getting her answer was more important. Her birthday was in November, and his was next April. "Ugh. That's—"

"Eight months." Willow shot him a crooked smile and studied her feet.

Blessed Orb, she knew the count? Did that mean she'd also been thinking of prebonding with him?

He was about to ask when Beri bounced over, grinning broadly.

"First time I've seen you smiling all day," Raven said. "Did you talk Salm into your chores in exchange for hauling his sister out of trouble?"

Beri thumped him on the back. "Merlin says we have passed our trials, no matter what else happens today. Brilliant example of *physical* teamwork, more than he could have hoped for!"

"Then you won't be using next year's pass?" Raven teased.

"I dinnae even need to attend this joust, he says."

"Aw…" Willow started.

"But I will, because I trust it will be safe."

Raven met Willow's gaze and smiled. This day was turning out all right. He elbowed Beri. "Maybe that trust advice isn't so bad."

ACKNOWLEDGMENTS

Trial at the Faire was written and revised during my 'stay home' spring and summer months of the 2020 COVID-19 pandemic. My thanks to my fellow zoom writers for quarantine cheer—I've checked in for daily writing sessions since March 2020. And thanks to my critiquing partners on CritiqueCircle.com, especially Tonin, Laura, Memy, Lizzie, Vickb, Edolan and Ace.

ABOUT THE AUTHOR

Before kids, Laurel Wanrow studied and worked as a naturalist —someone who leads wildflower walks and answers calls about the snake that wandered into your garage. During a stint of homeschooling, she turned her writing skills to fiction to share her love of the land, magical characters and fantastical settings.

She's the author of *The Luminated Threads* series, a Victorian historical fantasy mixing witches, shapeshifters and a sweet romance in a secret corner of England, and *The Windborne*, a nature-focused YA fantasy series set in our world.

When not living in her fantasy worlds, Laurel camps, hunts fossils, and argues with her husband and two new adult kids over whose turn it is to clean house. Though they live on the East Coast, a cherished family cabin in the Colorado Rockies holds Laurel's heart.

Visit her website at www.laurelwanrow.com.

facebook.com/laurelwanrowauthor

twitter.com/laurelwanrow

instagram.com/laurelwanrowauthor

bookbub.com/authors/laurel-wanrow

pinterest.com/laurelwanrow